CHINUA ACHEBE

THINGS FALL APART

Classics in Context

A carved wooden bowl for serving kola nuts to special guests

Heinemann Educational Publishers
Halley Court, Jordan Hill, Oxford OX2 8EJ
A part of Harcourt Education Limited

Heinemann: A Division of Reed Publishing (USA) Inc.
361 Hanover Street, Portsmouth, NH 03801–3912, USA

Heinemann Publishers (Pty) Limited
PO Box 781940, Sandton 2146, Johannesburg, South Africa

OXFORD MELBOURNE AUCKLAND
JOHANNESBURG KUALA LUMPUR GABORONE
PORTSMOUTH (NH) USA CHICAGO

Things Fall Apart © Chinua Achebe 1958
First published by William Heinemann Ltd, 1958
First published in the *African Writers Series* 1962
Illustrations to *Things Fall Apart* by Uche Okeke

First published with Introduction and Notes 1996
Reprinted 2000
Introduction © Simon Gikandi 1996
Introduction © Don C. Ohadike 1996
Selection and other Notes © Heinemann Educational Publishers 1996
Illustrations in the introduction by Priscilla Hinckley
Maps by John Gilkes

British Library Cataloguing in Publication Data
A catalogue record for this book is available from the British Library

Library of Congress Cataloguing-in-Publication data on
file at the Library of Congress

Cover design by Touchpaper
Cover illustration by Paul Wearing

ISBN 0 435 905 252

Phototypeset by CentraCet Limited, Cambridge
Printed and bound in Great Britain by
Cox & Wyman Ltd, Reading, Berkshire

03 04 05 06 19 18 17 16 15

Contents

Preface

Things Fall Apart was first published in 1958 and was reprinted in 1962 as the first novel in the African Writers Series. Nigerian writer Chinua Achebe portrays a stunning moment in African history – the imposition of colonial rule – with sympathy and dignity, focusing on the complexity and integrity of precolonial Igbo life, and the turmoil resulting from British rule. A 'classic' in every sense of the word, it has become the single best-known African novel around the globe, translated into at least 45 different languages.

While retaining the text of Achebe's manuscript and the original artwork by Uche Okeke, this new expanded edition includes additional material to help non-Igbo readers to better understand Achebe's classic in its social, historical, and literary context.

Simon Gikandi, a professor of literature at the University of Michigan and an acknowledged expert on Achebe's writing, has contributed an essay on 'Chinua Achebe and the Invention of African Literature.' Don Ohadike, an Igbo professor of African history at Cornell University, explains a great deal about 'Igbo Culture and History', while Priscilla Hinckley, an artist and educator who teaches African culture and the arts at Tufts University, has added a series of new illustrations in the front matter.

This new edition also includes a brief biography of Chinua Achebe, three maps of Nigeria and the Igbo area, a cast of characters in the novel, an expanded glossary of unfamiliar terms, and suggestions for further reading.

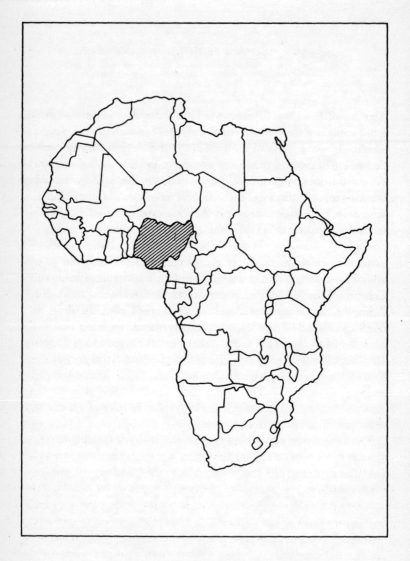

Map 1 Nigeria, one of the largest countries in Africa

Chinua Achebe: A Biographical Note

Born in 1930, Chinua Achebe was brought up in a pioneer Christian family in the large village of Ogidi, an early center of Anglican missionary work in Eastern Nigeria (and presumably a model for the fictional village of Umuofia). He attended a primary school run by the Church Missionary Society in Ogidi, and was later chosen to attend the Government College at Umuahia, considered among the best schools in West Africa. Recognized as an outstanding student, Achebe entered University College, Ibadan, in 1948, around the age of eighteen.

After studying literature at the University of Ibadan, he taught school for a year and then went to work for the Nigeria Broadcasting Company in Lagos. He had begun writing and publishing short stories during his university years, and followed those with the draft of a novel about the Nigerian encounter with colonialism seen through the lives of three generations within the same family. That long draft was ultimately divided into two parts, and published as *Things Fall Apart* (in 1958) and *No Longer At Ease* (in 1960). These were followed by *Arrow of God* in 1964.

Achebe's radio career ended abruptly in 1966 during the political upheavals that led to the Biafran War. He had narrowly escaped confrontation with armed soldiers, some of whom apparently believed that his 1966 novel, *A Man of the People*, implicated him in Nigeria's first military coup.

His career as a university academic began in 1967 with his appointment as Senior Research Fellow at the University of Nigeria. He was made Emeritus Professor in 1985. He has also taught at the University of Massachusetts and the University of Connecticut. Achebe has received numerous honors from different parts of the world, including over twenty honorary doctorates from universities in

Britain, the USA, Canada, and Nigeria. In 1987 he received Nigeria's highest award for intellectual achievement, the Nigerian National Merit Award.

Probably the most widely read of contemporary African writers, Achebe is the author of many novels, short stories, essays, and children's books. *Things Fall Apart*, his first novel, was first published in 1958. It had sold over 8 million copies by 1995. In the past two decades, Achebe's essays and lectures have stimulated international debate about the appropriate criteria by which African writers should be judged.

In addition to his own publishing career, Achebe helped to launch the career of many other African writers through his efforts as the original editor of the African Writers Series. *Things Fall Apart* was the first novel published in this series; during the first four decades of its existence, the series has included more than 350 titles.

Today Chinua Achebe lives in the USA, teaching at Bard College in New York. He is married and has four children.

Note to readers

The spelling 'Igbo' is used in the new material added to this edition, rather than the older form 'Ibo'; there is only a slight difference in pronunciation, a distinction most outsiders would not be able to hear.

Chinua Achebe and the Invention of African Literature

By Simon Gikandi

Although he is now considered to be the man who invented African literature, Chinua Achebe's goals were modest when he began to conceive and write *Things Fall Apart* in the early 1950s: 'I was quite certain that I was going to try my hand at writing, and one of the things that set me thinking was Joyce Cary's novel set in Nigeria, *Mister Johnson*, which was praised so much, and it was clear to me that this was a most superficial picture . . . and so I thought if this was famous, then perhaps someone ought to try and look at this from the inside' (*African Writers Talking*, 4). Achebe's project of looking at Nigerian culture from the inside was going to move more slowly than he might have expected, however. After sending the only copy of his manuscript to a typing agency in London where it was mislaid for nearly a year, he finally submitted his novel to William Heinemann, a famous British publisher of modern fiction. Heinemann did not welcome Achebe's novel without hesitation: not only was there no precedent for publishing modern African fiction, there were also concerns about its potential readership. Would there be many readers for a novel by an African writer dealing with the colonial encounter?

Ultimately, William Heinemann decided to take a chance on this new writer, and about 2,000 copies of the novel were published in 1958. The rest is history. *Things Fall Apart* is not only the most widely read African novel – the English edition alone has sold millions of copies – but is the one work of postcolonial literature that almost every student of English is bound to encounter at one time or another, often in high school, and most certainly in college and university.

But in thinking about the enormous success of this book and the influence it has had in the shaping of African and world literature, we

ix

should not forget its uncertain beginnings. Indeed, the history of this novel, which is also the history of the beginnings of modern African literature in English, is about how works of fiction create their own traditions, cultural contexts, and reading communities.

The first question any introduction to this novel must pose is this: what enabled Achebe's work to speak to its time in a way other novels could not? After all, *Things Fall Apart* was not the first African novel in English in the twentieth century. Achebe's novel was preceded by other important African novels such as Casely Hayford's *Ethiopia Unbound,* Sol Plaatje's *Mhudi,* and Amos Tutuola's *The Palm-Wine Drinkard.* If Achebe is now considered to be the man who invented African literature, it is not so much because he was a pioneer or an innovator. In the very simple and conventional story of Okonkwo, a strong individual and an Igbo hero struggling to maintain the cultural integrity of his people against the overwhelming power of colonial rule, Achebe was able to capture the anxieties of many African readers in the 1950s. We can understand these anxieties much better if we examine the important historical and psychological parallels between the years in which Okonkwo's story is set (between 1860 and 1890) and the years in which *Things Fall Apart* was conceived, written, and first published (1952–1958).

The central theme of the novel is what happens to the values that define Okonkwo's cultural community, and his own sense of moral order, when the institutions he had fought so hard to sustain collapse in the face of European colonialism. The cultural hero who had defeated Amalinze the Cat in the novel's first paragraph makes a regressive journey into exile and ultimate death. In retracing his rise and fall, we are also made aware of the collective dimension of his tragedy: Okonkwo may have failed because of his weaknesses as an individual, but his failure was inevitable because colonial rule had destabilized the values and institutions that sustained him. Indeed, there is a close relationship in the novel between Okonkwo's individual crisis – of authority and power – and the crisis of his community, which increasingly finds its defining characteristics (including notions of wealth, marriage, worship, language, and history) undermined and transplanted by the new colonial order. These issues are so powerful in the novel that attentive readers will rarely miss them.

Similarly, the period in which Achebe conceived and wrote *Things Fall Apart* was also a time of anxiety and crisis. By 1952 it had become apparent that the period of colonial rule in Nigeria was entering its final phase: after almost a hundred years of foreign domination, a period in which the culture of the country was often fashioned after that of Britain, and its destiny was often seen as somehow lying in Europe, the country was entering a period of self-government. And because this historical shift was as sudden as the initial imposition of colonial rule, critical questions arose: What was to be the nature of the Nigerian nation after colonialism? What kind of persons had colonial culture created? What was the language of the desired postcolonial culture? And, ultimately, how was the history and destiny of this new community to be charted?

Although *Things Fall Apart* may appear to be exclusively concerned with the imposition of colonial rule and the traumatic encounter between African and Europe, it is also a work that seeks to address the crisis of culture generated by the collapse of colonial rule. Indeed, Achebe has constantly argued that the theme of colonial domination in Africa – its rise and influence – was made imperative in his works by his concern that the culture of colonialism had had such a strong hold on African peoples, especially on a psychological level, that its consequences could continue to haunt African society long after European colonizers had left the continent. In one of his most influential statements on the role of the novelist in Africa, Achebe observed that, although decolonization had changed the African cultural landscape, it was foolish to pretend that Africans had 'fully recovered from the traumatic effects of our first confrontation with Europe' (*Morning Yet,* 44). Achebe went on to argue that his role as a writer was 'to help my society regain belief in itself and put away the complexes of the years of denigration and self-abasement' (*Morning Yet,* 44). In a situation in which colonial rule had established its authority by inventing and insisting on the racial inferiority of the African, novels set in the past, such as *Things Fall Apart*, were retrospective attempts to understand the origins of the current crisis – 'to look back and try and find out what went wrong, where the rain began to beat us' (*Morning Yet,* 44).

Clearly, the crisis of the soul triggered by colonialism at the end of

Things Fall Apart, when Okonkwo is forced to his death and his heroic life is reduced to a single paragraph in a racist European text, was very much an issue in 1958. However, unlike many other African writers of his generation, Achebe did not see colonial rule as something that could be transcended simply by an appeal to an heroic and romantic African past. And where other writers could see the culture of colonialism as the antithesis of an African identity, Achebe was interested in discovering a redemptive moment in colonialism, asking himself, in his own words, 'what possibility, what encouragement, there was in this episode of our history for the celebration of our own world, for the singing of the song of ourselves, in the din of an insistent world and song of others' (*Chinua Achebe: A Celebration,* 3).

Achebe's novel presents the colonial experience from an African perspective, but it does so without romanticizing the African past. Thus, one of the most enduring aspects of *Things Fall Apart* is Achebe's ambiguous representation of the Igbo past as heroic but, at the same time, compromised by Okonkwo's blind commitment to his culture and his obliviousness to alternative values and interpretations. This is the meaning of what is probably the definitive moment in the novel – the killing of Ikemefuna. Okonkwo strikes the fatal blow against his adopted son in the name of tradition and the moral order of his community but, as he is reminded by his friend Obierika, although the oracle of the hills (the custodian of moral authority) had decreed that the boy must be killed, she had not ordered Okonkwo, the surrogate father, to carry out the sentence. This one disturbing episode encapsulates the very essence of Achebe's philosophy, especially his concern with moral complexities and dualities. As he told Bill Moyers in a famous television interview, his values as a novelist are guided by a powerful Igbo proverb – 'Wherever something stands, something else will stand beside it' (*A World of Ideas,* 333). Culture is, in other words, defined by ambivalence rather than unquestioned authority.

If *Things Fall Apart* appears to be a novel that sets out to provide important moral lessons to its readers, it is because Achebe conceives the primary function – and power – of literature to be moral or ethical in nature. The power of the storyteller, says Achebe, lies in his or her ability to appeal to the mind and to reach beyond his or her particular circumstance and thus speak to different periods and generations; the good storyteller is not bound by narrow political or personal concerns or even by the demands of specific historical moments. Achebe's sympathies, then, are not with the heroic character (in this case Okonkwo), but the witness or storyteller (Obierika) who refuses to endorse Okonkwo's commitment to the central doctrines of his culture or the European colonizer's arrogant use of power.

However, the novelist's ability to bring the historical period and his moment of writing together also depended on a notable relationship between his life and his work. As an author, Achebe may be separated from the central events in *Things Fall Apart* by a period of seventy years, but his own biography is very much a part of the story he tells and its context. Achebe's family occupies a central role in the history which his novel narrates. We know, for example, that his great-grandfather was the man who first received Christian missionaries in the village of Ogidi (Umuofia in the novel). More significantly, Achebe's father, Isaiah Okafor (like Nwoye in the novel), was one of the first converts to Christianity in the area and worked for many years as an evangelist and teacher in the Christian Missionary Society, the evangelical branch of the Church of England. This family history is important to our understanding of *Things Fall Apart* not so much because it invites us to read the author's life in the novel itself, but because it calls attention to the cross-roads of culture from which Achebe's artistry emerges. For if the African identity of the novel derives from its acute sense of the oral tradition, then this is an acknowledgment of the influences of the Igbo stories which Achebe used to hear from his non-Christian relatives. It was from the older people in his village that Achebe came to develop an awareness of the history of Igbo people before colonization, a history which is an important aspect of the first part of *Things Fall Apart*.

But it would be a mistake to assume that Achebe grew up with a profound understanding and respect for the African past. One of the ironic aspects of being born in a family of African converts to Christianity was that one's status in society depended on a certain self-alienation from the old culture. 'The line between Christian and non-Christian was much more definite in my village forty years ago than it is today,' Achebe observed in 1973. 'When I was growing up I remember we tended to look down on the others. We were called in our language "the people of the church" or "the association of God." The others we called, with the conceit appropriate to followers of the true religion, the heathen or even "the people of nothing"' (*Morning Yet*, 65). Although Achebe's first novel is a celebration of the precolonial past, it is important to emphasize this sense of superiority among African Christians for one overwhelming reason: it was out of this identification with the culture of colonialism – and his ultimate disillusionment with it – that Achebe became a writer.

Achebe grew up and came of age in the culture of colonialism. He was not only brought up in a Christian family, and thus identified with European culture, his early education was in Church schools where the influence of the Bible and biblical stories, Christian moral codes, and indeed modern civility were emphasized. (Achebe has provided us with a wonderful portrait of this culture in the house of Isaac Okonkwo in his second novel, *No Longer at Ease*.) In addition, Achebe's secondary education at the prestigious government school at Umuahia could not but draw him even further into the culture of colonialism. Such schools were modeled after British public schools (the equivalent of prep schools in the United States) which meant that the values they promoted – in scholarship, sports, and conduct – were essentially English.

When he arrived at the University of Ibadan in 1948, Achebe was expected to read the major texts of the English tradition, including most notably Shakespeare, Milton, and Wordsworth. But by 1948 this acculturation in Englishness was being challenged by African nationalism: advocates of African independence and cultural renewal were beginning to question the central notion in colonial education – the assumption that an African destiny included 'a future European identity for which the present is but an apprenticeship'; in addition, the nationalist movement had brought about 'a mental revolution that was to reconcile us to ourselves' (*Morning Yet* 7, 70).

Since this mental revolution was connected so implicitly to the writing of *Things Fall Apart*, it is important that readers consider what we may call its cultural politics. Simply put, the writing of this novel marked a radical change in Achebe's way of looking at himself

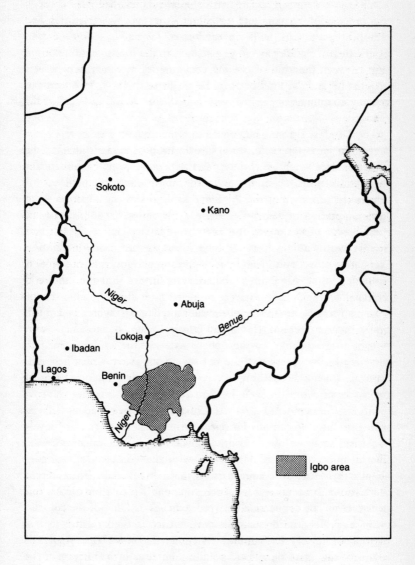

Map 2   Nigeria, showing the Igbo area

and his culture and in his conception of literature itself. For if we accept the general argument that colonial rule justified itself through the process of writing and rewriting other people's histories and cultural practices, as the last paragraph of *Things Fall Apart* seems to assert, then we must pay closer attention to the fundamental relationship between the kind of reading communities in which Achebe was brought up and the kind of novel he produced in 1958. Two forms of reading communities are involved: that of the family, and that of the school.

Achebe grew up in a household in which books were revered and played an important role in the visualization of modern life: 'As the fifth in a family of six children and with parents so passionate for their children's education, I inherited many discarded books ... I remember also my mother's *Ije Onye Kraist* which must have been an Igbo adaptation of *Pilgrim's Progress*' (*Morning Yet*, 68). Many of these books, most notably the Bible, were later to influence Achebe's literary works as much as the Igbo stories he heard as a child. The Ikemefuna episode in *Things Fall Apart*, to cite just one example, is fashioned after Abraham's aborted sacrifice of Isaac in the Old Testament.

In high school, as Achebe observed later, he was exposed to English books such as *Treasure Island* and *Oliver Twist*. The most significant impact of these books was on Achebe's view of the world: on reading these books, he observes, 'I did not see myself as an African to begin with ... I went through my first level of schooling thinking I was of the party of white man in his hair-raising adventures and narrow escapes' (*Chinua Achebe*, 7). At University College Ibadan, Achebe was introduced to famous European writers who had set their novels in Africa, such as Joseph Conrad, Joyce Cary, and Graham Greene. But by now, instead of identifying with the European adventurers against their African counterparts, Achebe felt impelled to represent the historical encounter between Europe and Africa from an African perspective. The connection between Achebe's reading of the colonial novel and his decision to become a writer is fundamental to our understanding of the cultural function of *Things Fall Apart*: 'I suddenly saw that these books had to be read in a different light. Reading *Heart of Darkness*, for instance, ... I realized that I was one of those savages jumping up and down on the beach. Once that kind of enlightenment comes to you, you realize that someone has to write a different story' (*A World of Ideas*, 343).

Things Fall Apart is certainly not the first African novel, but it was probably the first work in which the author set out to represent the African experience in a narrative that sought, self-consciously, to be different from the colonial novel. Since its publication in 1958, Achebe's novel has served as a model for other African writers, and indeed, for a different kind of literature in English. Achebe's goal in this novel – to indicate to his readers 'that we in Africa did not hear of culture for the first time from Europeans' (*African Writers Talking* 7) – has changed the way African readers perceive their own cultures and their relationship to colonial institutions. Achebe is the man who invented African literature because he was able to show, in the structure and language of his first novel, that the future of African writing did not lie in simple imitation of European forms but in the fusion of such forms with oral traditions. Achebe is the conscience of African literature because he has consistently insisted on the power of storytellers to appeal to the morality and humanity of their readers and to give their life fuller meaning.

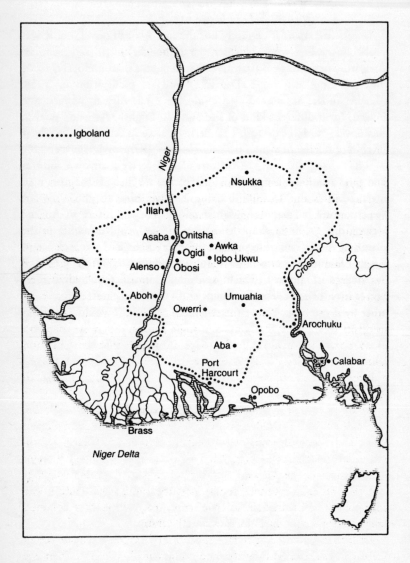

.... Igboland

Niger

Nsukka •

Illah •

Asaba • • Onitsha
• Ogidi • Awka
Alenso • • Igbo Ukwu
• Obosi

Aboh • Umuahia •
Owerri •

Cross

Arochuku

Aba •

Port
Harcourt • Calabar •

Opobo •

Brass

Niger Delta

Map 3   Igboland, showing the major places listed in the text

Igbo Culture and History

By Don C. Ohadike

Early Igbo History

The Igbo (or Ibo) people form one of the largest ethnic groups in Africa, with about 15 million living in Nigeria and another million living outside. Their farming communities are broadly situated between the Niger River in the west and the Cross River in the east, stretching from delta swampland near the southern coast through tropical rain forest to open grasslands to the north. The Igbo language has dozens of dialects, which developed because Igboland was an aggregation of self-contained towns and villages, separated from each other by dense bush. Before the twentieth century, it would have been incorrect to speak of the Igbo as a single people; they were made up of over two hundred separate groups. Although their customs and languages were clearly related, each group could have been considered a distinct society, encompassing perhaps twenty or thirty villages. An Igbo person who traveled thirty miles in Igboland might have had great difficulty making himself or herself understood. However, during the colonial period (1900–1960) many Igbo people ventured far from home and congregated in urban centers, at the work place, and in institutions of higher learning. Many realized that what they thought were distinct languages were different dialects of the same language and that all Igbo-speaking people had the same basic culture and sociopolitical organization. In that sense, the concept of a common Igbo identity is a product of the twentieth century.

An Igbo creation myth relates that in the beginning the surface of the earth was covered by water and no humans lived on it. Then one day Chukwu (God) created the first human family, composed of Eze

A man and his wives receive a gift of yams from their
daughter's husband

Nri, his wife, his sons, and his daughters. Eze Nri and his family stood on the top of an anthill and had nowhere to go because the land was submerged. They were also hungry. Chukwu looked down and took pity on their condition. He gave Eze Nri a piece of yam and said, 'Take this, it is edible.' Eze Nri and his family ate the yam and found it was good.

The following morning, they were hungry again and Eze Nri prayed to God for more yam. Chukwu listened attentively and then gave him some yam seeds, saying, 'Plant these and you will have an abundance of yams.' Eze Nri accepted the yam seeds with gratitude. He looked around him and said to Chukwu, 'But the land is covered with water.' Chukwu instructed him to send for Awka blacksmiths, who came with their bellows and blew until the land was dry. Chukwu then asked Eze Nri to sacrifice his first son and his first daughter and plant the yam seeds in their graves. Eze Nri obeyed. Shortly afterwards, yam and cocoyam tendrils sprouted from his children's graves. Eventually, Eze Nri harvested yams and cocoyams and shared them among the Igbo people.

This story establishes the Igbo people's belief in a supreme god (Chukwu) who created all things and demanded obedience. It also suggests that religion has long been an integral part of Igbo life. The myth points to the origins of agriculture, the antiquity of the family, and the importance of iron working in shaping the Igbo community. Above all, since this myth makes no mention of migrations from distant places – as opposed to the majority of African traditions of origin – it suggests that the Igbo people have occupied their present locale for a very long time, a suggestion that is confirmed by archaeology.

Archaeological evidence shows today's Igbo people and their ancestors have been settled in roughly the same geographical region for two thousand years or more. Much of the material culture of present-day Igbo people resembles that of the people who occupied certain locations in Igboland around 1,000 BC. At Afikpo, present-day pottery resembles that produced about 3,000 years ago. At one of the Afikpo sites, the number of stone implements gradually decreased as the amount and variety of pottery increased, showing the transition from hunting and gathering to agriculture.

Igbo people have smelted and forged iron for centuries, and their oral traditions are rich with accounts of iron working and iron use. At Lejja, a small town situated about ten miles south of Nsukka, an ancient iron-working settlement existed where smelting was done in a pit or bowl furnace, initially using rather primitive techniques. Over time, the Igbo improved their technological skills and began to produce sophisticated metal tools such as spearheads, arrowheads, swords, hoes, knives, earrings, finger rings, bracelets, anklets, hammers, anvils, tweezers, scissors, and cooking pots. By the first millennium of the Christian era, they were already producing bronze masks and figurines, of the types that archaeologists discovered in Igbo-Ukwu.

The widespread use of iron tools enabled the Igbo people to make better use of the forest. With iron tools they grew yams (their principal staple food), cocoyams, bananas, and plantains. Iron tools also helped them to cut down fruits from the tall palm trees, and process them into edible and medicinal oils. Scholars have attributed the current high density of the Igbo population to the antiquity and effectiveness of yam cultivation and their skills at exploiting the oil palm.

At its fully developed stage, the Igbo agricultural system was based on shifting cultivation, a type of rotating cultivation where the same fields were planted for several years in succession and then were left fallow to regain their fertility. Crops did best on forest land cleared for the first time, but some people, either unwilling or unable to handle the back-breaking amount of work required to clear virgin forest, planted their yams continuously on old farm lands and reaped poor harvests as a result. In *Things Fall Apart*, Okonkwo's father is portrayed as too lazy to clear forest land; he prays to the spirits to grant him a better harvest but is rebuked for his own lack of initiative.

Social and Political Structures

A striking feature of Igbo society was the lack of centralized political structures. The Igbo lived in autonomous villages and towns, ruled by their elders. With a few exceptions, they organized themselves in patrilineages – lineage groups organized along lines of descent from father to son. Relationships were based on blood ties, and each person traced his or her descent to three groups. First, a person belonged to the smallest social unit known as *uno*, or house. This was a natural family, consisting of a man, his wife or wives, and their children. The second group was the *umunna*, or lineage, composed of a number of related houses. Finally, a group of lineages formed a compact village or town, *obodo*. This was the highest territorially defined authority of the Igbo. A town or compact village was sometimes named after its founder, or after a striking geographical feature that best described its location. It might also be named after the most important sociological circumstances that surrounded its foundation. It is important to recognize that the members of a lineage were blood relatives and that each lineage was a semi-autonomous unit within a town. Each house, lineage, and town was headed by a headman, *onyisi*, who acquired the position by virtue of his age. Town meetings were usually held in the town square, but the most important lineage and house meetings were held in the *obi* (meeting shed) of the most senior elders. Interaction between towns was limited and was regulated by goodwill, mutual respect, and diplomacy. Wars often broke out when these failed.

Cross-cutting Ties
The Igbo communities were known as extremely democratic, yet they had no centralized governments. How, then, did they achieve democracy?

The Igbo subscribed to the principle of direct participation in government. Their entire social and political structures revolved around the idea of cross-cutting ties. The five most important cross-cutting institutions were the councils of elders, age-groups, councils of chiefs, women's associations, and secret societies. Without them, the Igbo society would be starved of its essence and would disintegrate. As we shall presently see, the traditional Igbo communities did indeed fall apart in the twentieth century when the Europeans destroyed their cross-cutting ties in the process of colonial rule.

Council of Elders
Matters affecting lineage members were discussed at the meetings of its elders, *ndisi* or *indichie,* with the assistance of the adult members

The beautifully carved door of a senior man

of the lineage. In inter-lineage disputes, elders from the affected lineages met to discuss solutions, with the oldest man in the gathering presiding.

The authority of the lineage head derived from the group's respect for him as the oldest living representative of the founding ancestors. He was the custodian of ancestral lands, the keeper of the ritual objects that symbolized political authority, and the group's spiritual and temporal head. Even though he was the religious, executive, and judicial head of his lineage, he would not act without their approval. No action would be taken until an issue had been fully argued at a lineage meeting and some degree of consensus achieved.

Age-groups

An age-group association, known as *ogbo* or *otu*, was composed of men (or women) who were of about the same age. All residents of a town born within a few years of each other belonged to the same age-group, with separate sections for men and women. The association was named after a major event that was taking place at the time of its members' birth. For example, there were the Biafran War age-group, *ogbo aya Biafra* (those born between 1967 and 1970), the Second World War age-group, *ogbo aya Hitler* (1939–1945), and the influenza age-group, *ogbo ifelunza* (1918–1921). The exact age-span in an age-group varied from town to town, but the most common were the three- and five-year intervals.

The age-group system enabled societies without written records to remember past events. It also helped them assign special duties and responsibilities to the different segments of the community, in accordance with the principle of seniority.

The junior age-groups (age 15 and below) did minor jobs like fetching water, cleaning footpaths, sweeping the streets and town squares, and running errands.

Men in the middle age-groups (from about age 16 to about 40) formed the fighting forces. If five years separated one age-group from the next, there would be up to five distinct age-groups in this category. In the event of a war, each age-group acted as a separate regiment, under a leader who belonged to an older age-group. The middle age-groups also felled trees and cleared the bush at the beginning of each planting season. They functioned as the executive arm of the government and would apprehend fugitives, for example. After marriage, young women would become active in the appropriate women's association (see below).

The senior male age-groups (those aged 40 and above) were responsible for judicial matters. They usually decided when a town should go to war, how an offender should be punished, when the various agricultural cycles would open and close, and when the annual festivals would be held.

The age-group system promoted respect. Juniors deferred to seniors and expected the same treatment when they advanced to higher grades. The members of a group acted together, and the friendships they cultivated in childhood remained intact throughout life.

The Acquisition of Titles and the Council of Chiefs

The Igbo people emphasized personal achievement; hereditary succession to titles would have contradicted notions of leadership and fair play. Some Igbo men managed to acquire prestigious titles, enabling them to be acknowledged as great men or chiefs. Titled chiefs formed their own councils and represented their communities to outsiders.

Most Igbo men eagerly sought admission into the council of chiefs, but not all could succeed. Every Igbo man began his life as an apprentice. A young boy accompanied his father or uncle to the farm and rendered as much assistance as he could. As he grew older he learned that marriage, wealth, and the acquisition of titles enabled individuals to advance socially. Until a man was initiated into certain titles, he could not dress in certain ways, or wear hats of certain colors, or shake hands in certain ways, or take a piece of kola nut before other people.

Titles cost money; only men with exceptional abilities and good luck ever bought all the available titles. The taking of the higher titles demanded the payment of expensive initiation fees, accompanied by elaborate feasting and dancing. Throughout Igboland, a man who failed to progress beyond the most junior titles was a man without status in the eyes of his people. Whatever his age, they looked upon him as a boy. His age mates might make him run errands for them. In

Awka he might be termed *agbala,* a woman. In Illah, he was taunted, *isi igwu,* meaning, 'head full of lice,' or 'louse breeder.' When he died, they buried him without dignity, and the mourning period was brief. Status attainment was clearly linked to the acquisition of wealth through hard work.

The highest title in many Igbo communities (and the one alluded to in Okonkwo's village) was *ozo* (or any of its variants: *eze, nze, alo,* and *ichie).* To qualify for the *ozo* title, a man must have acquired the junior titles and discharged all the duties normally assigned to members of the junior title groups. He must have accumulated enough wealth and completed the ceremonies connected with the second burial of his father. Thus, no man could attain a status that might equal or exceed his father's while the latter was still alive.

The Igbo believed that no man could inherit immortality; it must be acquired through a process of title-taking called *ichi-echichi,* 'to secure the breath of life', to attain immortality or godship. The Igbo word *chi* represents invisible forces, spirits, and personal gods; it is the root of such words as Chukwu (God), *ichie,* an immortal or a titled person, and *ndi ichie,* title holders.

Only men who achieved this ritual death and resurrection could attain immortality; an *ozo* man was a person who had received the gift of immortality. He was no longer an ordinary human, but a god. To purchase the highest title was, therefore, to be born again, to be admitted into the association of rulers, *otu ochichi,* and to be initiated into the cult of the ancestors, *otu ndichie.*

At the secular level, the highest title spared its holder the indignity of manual labor. It guaranteed him a seat in the council of chiefs. It reserved for him portions of fees paid by new initiates into the title association and gave him rights to certain portions of livestock slaughtered in his lineage. A titled man was greeted with high-sounding salutations such as *igwe* (His Highness) and *ogbu efi* (he who slaughters bulls). The *ozo* title lost its appeal in the twentieth century when colonial officers stripped traditional Igbo chiefs of their power and then subordinated them to British-appointed warrant chiefs and Western-educated Africans.

Women's Associations

Igbo women had their own clubs, age-group associations, and title associations that complemented those of men. Women controlled certain spheres of community life, just as men controlled other spheres. Women were perceived to possess superior spiritual well-being and headed many of the traditional cults and shrines. In Achebe's novel, for example, the oracle is served by a priestess. Women also gained status by amassing wealth through trading, farming, or weaving, and were treated as *ndi ogalanya,* wealthy persons. In certain districts, wealthy women married other women, and 'fathered' their own children.

Like an Igbo man, every Igbo woman began her life as an apprentice. From a very young age a girl assisted her mother at home, on the farm, or in the marketplace. As she grew older she learned from experience that hard work, marriage, and membership of certain associations enabled women to advance socially. One of the most important women's associations was *otu omu* (the Omu society), headed by a female functionary, known as Omu. The desire to join this prestigious association acted as an incentive for hard work and thrift, for only women who had enough wealth to pay for the initiation ceremonies were admitted. The members of the Omu society acted as a pressure group in political matters and imposed fines on men and women who disturbed the peace of the marketplace. They punished quarrelsome women and those who broke certain taboos, like those prohibiting incest and adultery. It was perilous for any man, no matter how influential, to provoke the anger of this association.

The leaders of the Omu society attended the meetings of the councils of chiefs and elders and participated in discussions affecting the welfare of the citizens. Though they would not themselves take part in wars, they could decide when to urge the male warrior chiefs to start one.

The Omu society and several other women's associations, acted as checks and balances in the social and political organization of Igbo communities. The *otu umu ada* was an association of women born to a lineage or town, while *otu inyeme di* was an association of women married to the men of a lineage or town. In theory, every married woman belonged to both associations, while an unmarried woman belonged only to *otu umu ada*. Whereas men participated in the

An elaborate coiffure for a girl whose marriage is being negotiated

politics of their home towns alone, women exercised influence in the politics of both their home towns and the towns of their marriage.

Of special importance was the control women exercised over local trade. In the Igbo world view, a marketplace was not simply a place to buy and sell goods; it was also a ritual, political, and social center. The power women exercised over the organization of local trade derived from the fact that most local traders were women. They alone could best serve the needs of those who converged in the marketplace for commercial and other purposes. Caravans of long-distance traders made their way to local markets, often accompanied by a large number of noncommercial specialists, such as the agents of important oracles, smiths, carvers, priests, diviners, and doctors. Although most long-distance traders were men, their prosperity depended upon the careful regulation of local markets. Igbo women's associations upheld gender balance and equality. Their political and social activities were very useful, though men occasionally felt they were contentious.

Secret Societies

Some secret societies were exclusively for men, some for women, and others for both sexes. Very little is known about the secret societies because the men and women who joined them took their oath of secrecy very seriously. Besides, the Igbo were averse to divulging information that might hinder the effectiveness of their secret societies; many of them functioned as the mouthpieces of ancestors, oracles, and spirits. In important judicial matters, masked ancestors (the *egwugwu*, or *egungun*) might appear and pronounce a verdict. In Chapter Ten of *Things Fall Apart*, for example, we see the *egwugwu* emerge to hear a series of legal cases. When that happened, no one contested their judgment, because no one could pretend to be wiser than the ancestors or the spirits. And no one ever disclosed the identity of the individual behind the mask, even if he happened to recognize the voice or the walk of a particular elder.

Igbo Marriage Customs

Marriage also served to bring households, lineages, and even towns together. The Igbo regarded it as the cornerstone of their whole social structure. Discussions leading to marriage were taken seriously, and they involved not just the immediate families of the bride and groom

A masked figure, representing an ancestral spirit

but also their entire lineages. The Igbo believed that every adult male and female must marry and build their own household. They valued children very highly, and marriage was a requisite first step towards bringing them into the world.

The key unit of agricultural production was the household. In the absence of mechanization, the size of a household was crucial in providing enough labor. Realizing that monogamy was a sure avenue to poverty, most husbands practiced polygamy. If a man failed to act promptly to increase the size of his household, his wife might bring additional wives to him.

Having several women in a household enhanced not only a man's status but also the prestige of the first wife. As the head woman of the household, she shared every title that the man might acquire. She presided over household deliberations, most men preferring not to get personally involved, except in emergencies. Junior wives enjoyed the security and prosperity that large households provided. In addition, Igbo women had rights and freedoms that they jealously guarded. They lived in their own separate houses, cooked for themselves, and raised their own children. They grew crops, part of which they sold in the marketplace, and kept the proceeds. Moreover, Igbo laws and customs permitted an unhappy wife to leave.

Igbo Religion

The line that separated the religious life from the secular in Igbo culture was as thin as air. The Igbo believed in the Supreme Being (Chukwu) and in life after death. Chukwu lived far away in the sky; he was the origin of all things and directed the activities of all things. The names the Igbo gave their children expressed these beliefs. For example, an Igbo family might name a baby Amaogechukwu ('God's time is the best'), or Chukwukelu ('God is the creator'), or Chukwunyelu ('God gave me this wonderful gift').

Moreover, Igbo proverbs, folk tales, and incantations testified to their belief in the existence of God. Since nothing happened by chance, everything – good health or illness, fortune or misfortune – was attributed to the will of God. They also believed that one must live in peace with one's ancestors to be rewarded with good health, good luck and many children. Misfortune and untimely death were consequences of living in disharmony with the higher beings.

Igbo people had no symbols of Chukwu because no one knew what he looked like. They rarely kept special altars or shrines for his worship, since he was everywhere at the same time. Every transgression was ultimately an offense against him, and they constantly prayed that those trespasses that they might unknowingly have committed be forgiven them. The Igbo people nursed a deep reverence for the mysterious nature of Chukwu. They were not sure how to approach him, but they knew that he was a spirit and that those who worshipped him must do so in spirit. They therefore communed with him through the major spirits and ancestors.

The Igbo also believed in the existence of the Ekwensu, the equivalent of Satan, whose prime occupation was to lead people astray. Ekwensu had several servants who helped him carry out his evil thoughts. One of them was death itself, the malicious being who would visit a man on the day he enjoyed life the most.

Ekwensu used people to commit crimes against other people and would then turn around and punish the same people who served him. Ekwensu was Chukwu's principal enemy and at the same time his faithful servant. Acting on the powers bestowed on him by Chukwu, he would cause an evil doer to suffer or die in a strange manner. Should a man meet with an unexpected misfortune, it was a punishment for some crime he had committed. The crime might have escaped the attention of his neighbors but not the watchful eyes of the higher forces. Until a sinner atoned for a transgression he might not even remember committing, he remained in a state of conflict with the higher forces, who would punish him continuously. When a person felt disturbed by certain inexplicable misfortunes, he would approach a diviner, who might recommend that the unseen forces be propitiated. Fear of unconsciously offending the higher beings was responsible for the large number of propitiation rites.

The Igbo also approached the higher forces when they wanted special favors. Should a family want to have many children, it would approach a diviner who might recommend some sacrificial offerings. Sacrifice was an important element in Igbo religious ceremony.

Igbo people had a wide range of spirit symbols that often took the form of natural phenomena. Among these were spirits of the rivers, streams, lakes, rain, hills, caves, lightning, iron, the farm, the earth, strength, fertility, and witchcraft. A spirit symbol might have its own priest or priestess. Certain professions had their own patron gods who assisted them in their endeavors. A patron god might be connected to rain making, hunting, farming, trading, or iron working. For example, by offering the right sacrifices, prayers and invocations, a rain maker could persuade the rain god to produce rain.

Rivers, streams, lakes, and rain had life-sustaining qualities, and symbolized purity, cleanliness, coolness, freshness, fertility, and longevity. The water spirits were important deities. With water, the Igbo washed away evil and uncleanness. Important cleansing rituals were performed near, or in, rivers and streams.

The most dreaded spirits were associated with fire (*oku*) and thunder *(amadioha* or *akpala)*. Fire symbolized raging flames, burning heat, burning forests, dryness, drought, bad harvest, high fever, miscarriage in pregnant women, and death. When a community indulged in excessive sin, its territory might become a fiery surface, and humans, livestock and plants might die. Only qualified doctors could cool the land again.

Any object could be turned into an object of worship if consecrated. Even after its consecration, the object would never acquire the qualities of a god, nor would it ever become a god; instead it would become a religious object, assuming the name of the spirit it represented. Its power would depend on the strength of the spirit that lived in it. A body of water, a piece of metal, a stone, or even a piece of bone might serve as an object of worship; however, it is not the stone or bone that is being worshipped; but rather the spirit that it represented. Many outsiders have jumped to the conclusion that the object is the god itself.

The most common object of worship was *ikenga*, a wooden carving, that symbolized a man's strength and success, distinguished by its prominent horns. Anyone could buy an *ikenga* in the marketplace and have a qualified priest invoke the right spirit into it, after which it would acquire the strength of the spirit it held. Until the necessary act of invocation had been performed, it remained a mere object. Every

Igbo household had an *ikenga*. A man never parted with his *ikenga*, although he might replace one destroyed by fire, for example. He consulted his *ikenga* before he embarked on any project, and he would offer libation in its name whenever he served palm wine in his house.

Of equal standing was a man's personal god, *chi*. *Chi* was similar to the Christian concept of a guardian angel. A person's *chi* followed him or her throughout life, and could be either benevolent or malignant. A person with a good *chi* was always successful in his or her endeavors, while a person with a bad *chi* was an unfortunate person, who would labor without reaping.

The Igbo people did not believe that a man's *chi* controlled his entire destiny. No matter how 'good' his *chi* was, a person would achieve success only if he worked hard and led an upright life. They emphasized the importance of hard work in the saying 'If a person says "yes", that person's *chi* says "yes".' In addition, the Igbo believed that diviners and other medicine men and women could intervene on behalf of an unfortunate person to change his or her malignant *chi* into a benevolent one. Most private prayers, sacrifices, and invocations were directed toward chasing off misfortune and keeping oneself in a state of harmony with one's *chi*.

At the group level, one of the chief deities of the Igbo people was Ani, the earth deity, the great mother goddess, and the spirit of fertility. Every lineage and, indeed, every homestead had a shrine dedicated to her. Ani had her own special priestesses, who played leading roles in many aspects of community life. They officiated during all religious ceremonies that concerned Ani and presided over all matters involving crime against the earth goddess. Their presence was vital when matters concerning incest, birth, death, and burial were being discussed. The ultimate resting place for all men and women who had led a good life was in the bosom of Ani. On the other hand, all men and women who practiced witchcraft or died a shameful death, including those who committed suicide, had no place in Ani's abode. Usually their corpses were left unburied in the 'bad bush.'

Like some other belief systems, the entire religious system of the Igbo people revolved around the idea of birth, death, and reincarnation. The Igbo believed that when elders died their spirits did not go away for good, but prowled unseen, looking after the welfare of the living members of the lineage. An elder would pour libations to his departed forebears before he drank his palm wine. He would also give a piece of kola nut in their name as he asked for their protection and guidance. The Igbo often offered animal sacrifices in the names of departed ancestors. If a baby boy was born soon after the death of his grandfather, this child could have been no other person than the old man reincarnated and might be named Nnamdi or Nnadi ('Father is back'). If a baby girl was born soon after the death of her grandmother, she might be named Nnenna.

The Igbo people believed that infants could also be reincarnated, but these babies usually put their parents through unnecessary pain. Babies often died soon after birth only to come back again to the same parents, as a result of which they were called *ogbanje,* meaning those who 'come and go.' Some women were known to have lost up to five children, none of them living long enough to witness the birth of the next child. To break this circle of birth and death, a diviner would have to be consulted. In Achebe's novel, Ezinma's mother has buried nine of her ten children; she is desperately afraid that Ezinma too will prove to be an *ogbanje.*

The Enigma of Twinship
Until the beginning of the twentieth century, the Igbo threw away twin babies soon after they were born. People today are very reluctant to talk about it, for they cannot explain why they often prayed to God (Chukwu) for many children, yet when twins or triplets were born, the infants were left in the forest to die. This was not an Igbo phenomenon alone, however. Many African groups regarded the birth of twins as supernaturally charged and took different steps to deal with it. For example, the San people of southern Africa would destroy one or both babies. Among the Ashanti, the babies would be forfeited to the chief; their parents would place them in a brass basin, and then carry them to the chief's palace soon after birth. On the other hand, twins born into the royal family were killed at once to prevent the confusion and turmoil their birth might cause in terms of succession and inheritance.

The Igbo believed that there was something abnormal and mystical about twins. When people ask for rain, they do not expect a flood; twin birth represented excessive fertility and had to be kept in check. After leaving the babies in the bush to die, the mother would undergo extensive rituals intended to prevent her from bearing more twins. If appropriate measures were not immediately taken, not only the parents of twins but the entire community might suffer harm.

Homicide

Spilling the blood of a townsman or townswoman was a serious offense against the earth goddess. However, criminal justice systems varied, especially in regard to how law breakers were punished. For example, whereas most Igbo groups would hang a murderer, in certain towns a husband who killed his wife was hanged, while a woman who killed her husband was not. In some towns a woman who killed her co-wife was not hanged, because both women belonged to the same man.

If a murder occurred in precolonial times, certain age-groups might seize the property of the murderer and destroy his house. If he ran away, they might hold his relatives hostage until the murderer was brought in and hanged. In other areas, if a murderer escaped, a waiting period of three or more years was allowed, after which his lineage paid a fine and gave one of their daughters to the family of the dead man. These examples demonstrate the Igbo people's abhorrence for blood-letting. Accidental homicide might attract a lighter punishment, but no killing ever went unpunished. Of equal importance was the principle that restitution must be made to the victim's relatives.

Killing was permitted only during war, but combatants made every effort to keep casualties to the minimum. Even in war, killing another was a transgression against the earth goddess, Ani. Cutting off the heads of one's enemies, practiced by certain Igbo groups and bragged about by Okonkwo in the novel, was neither accepted nor practiced by the majority of Igbo people. When men returned from war, they performed elaborate cleansing rituals before they could rejoin their lineages. Homicide was only one item in a long list of acts treated as abomination, nso. When an act of abomination was committed, a qualified doctor had to be brought in at once to remove it. An offender, together with his or her kin group and the wider community, would remain in a state of ritual turbulence until these rituals were completed.

Igbo Oracles

Straddling the religious and secular worlds were the Igbo oracles. Oracles were religious shrines that discharged both judicial and oracular functions and acted as centers for divination. They received messages from dead relatives and passed them on to the living. They explained to curious relatives why a person had died. They warned individuals and whole communities about impending danger and offered advice on ritual matters. A community might consult an oracle if disturbed by a high death rate, or an unduly high rate of twin births, or successive bad harvests. Oracles also acted as courts of appeal in judicial matters. Individuals might take their dispute to an oracle if they failed to reconcile their differences. If a man felt that he had been wrongfully accused of a crime, he might take the matter to an oracle, who might exonerate him or confirm the guilt.

Oracles were feared and respected for miles around; one example was that of the Aro oracle, known to Europeans as the Long Juju. The Aro oracle was consulted by traders from many areas to settle business disputes. Oracles were housed in secret groves, surrounded by thick bush. The home of an oracle was a forbidden territory, for the Igbo believed that anyone who saw an oracle would surely die. Only the chief priestess (or priest) ever looked upon the face of the oracle; supplicants never approached an oracle directly. The chief priestess of an oracle served as the mouthpiece of the deity that dwelt in the shrine. Her words were final in all matters, because the forces she represented were higher than all secular powers. To disobey the orders of the priestess was to disobey the deity she represented. The chief priestess might combine her oracular services with other vocations like trading or farming. She and her agents received gifts of money, foodstuffs, and livestock for their services, and they might demand certain sacrifices as well.

The Igbo believed that their oracles would offer impartial decisions in judicial matters. So great was the confidence they reposed in their oracles that they would willingly pay large sums of money to consult them and accept whatever verdict they might pronounce. Most of the agents of the oracles traveled far and wide as medicine men, diviners, traders, smiths, or carvers. They used their knowledge of the communities they visited to direct litigants to the oracles they represented.

Up to this point, I have presented a rather generalized description of Igbo society before the coming of the Europeans. We must remember that the Igbo clans were numerous and autonomous, and there were many variations in culture and political systems deriving from their relative isolation from one another and their different relations with such neighboring kingdoms as Benin, Igala, Ijo, Efik, and Urhobo. What one town permitted might be forbidden in another. Despite these variations, the Igbo people shared certain basic cultural attributes that set them apart from other groups in West Africa. Isolation ceased to be a factor in the twentieth century, following the spread of wage labor and the construction of motor roads and railway lines, but even before that external influence intensified when Igboland was flooded with European immigrants and their African employees. In the pages that follow we examine how the European presence drastically modified Igbo society.

The Igbo People Meet the Europeans: The Era of Informal Empire

The Igbo people's meeting with the Europeans in the nineteenth century would change their history. European slave traders had exported substantial numbers of Igbo people from the Bight of Biafra to the New World. Nonetheless, no European had penetrated the interior of Igboland before 1830.

The events that led to the establishment of a European presence in Igboland were tied to the politics of abolition. Realizing that the slave trade was no longer consistent with their economic interests, the British, who had dominated the trade, championed the movement that eventually brought it to a close. While the abolition debate raged on, however, certain interest groups in Europe and America formed societies to push European cultural, commercial, and political influence into the African interior. One of the most famous was the African

Association, which sponsored many expeditions into Africa. Expeditions such as those led by Mungo Park, Hugh Clapperton, and Richard and John Lander reassured the British public that the Niger River emptied itself into the Atlantic Ocean and that European traders had done business in the coastal towns at the mouth of the river for over three centuries. Encouraged by these successes, the British government and private organizations sent further expeditions up the Niger River to establish contacts with the Africans of that region. These Niger expeditions were undertaken by missionaries and traders, sometimes accompanied by government officials.

Between 1832 and 1854, expeditions up the Niger River risked devastation by tropical diseases. The West African interior came to be described as the 'white man's grave'. The expeditions continued despite these risks. In 1854 medical workers confirmed that the use of quinine minimized death from malaria, and other advances in medicine and technology facilitated further European penetration.

The increasing European demand for palm oil and an expanding African demand for imported European goods encouraged the British to establish trading posts in Aboh, Onitsha, and Lokoja in 1857. Pleased with the booming trade, some Igbo communities invited European traders and missionaries to come and live among them.

Friendly relations began to crumble after 1875, however, when the palm oil business entered a long period of economic depression. Palm oil prices fell in Europe while the prices of manufactured goods were on the rise, leading to trade disputes between European and African traders. Conflict also developed around the question of security on the Niger. African chiefs had developed a system of trade that guaranteed peace along the Niger River and on the mainland. The chiefs of the various states collected tolls, duties, or tributes from passing traders; European traders initially paid the tributes because they needed the protection of local chiefs. When British gunboats began to ply the Niger River more frequently in the 1880s, however, European traders began to refuse to pay these tolls, arguing that the chiefs did not provide adequate protection. The chiefs relaxed security, and some private citizens took advantage of the situation to organize widespread robberies, sometimes attacking European trading posts and vessels. Obviously, such actions and the retaliation they often provoked strained relationships and generated violence along the river. This period is often described in terms of 'gunboat diplomacy'.

For some time the British government ignored the appeal of British traders for military assistance. In October 1879, however, in response to a complaint that some citizens of Onitsha had attacked British citizens, the British War Office authorized Captain Burr to bombard the town. Captain Burr anchored the warship *Pioneer* midstream and opened fire. After bombarding Onitsha for two days, Captain Burr led his men into the town, where they 'destroyed every object' they could find. The warriors of Onitsha bravely defended their town but were no match for the better-armed British.

The British justified their action on the grounds that the chiefs were unable to control their subjects, and that it was appropriate for British 'moral force' to curb acts of violence against British subjects. Again in 1883, three British warships shelled and destroyed Aboh, on the charge that some Aboh citizens had attacked a British trader.

The Missionary Factor
Having protected its traders with warships, the British government could no longer ignore the plight of its missionaries, who also demanded assistance. Protecting the missionaries was far more difficult, however; while traders confined their activities to the banks of the Niger River, Christian missionaries carried their propaganda further inland, provoking indignation among the inhabitants.

The role of Christian missionaries in the conquest of Africa is sometimes underestimated. Missionaries were the first foreigners to venture inland in fairly large numbers, and their accounts of what they found helped stimulate imperial ambitions. Such missionaries played an important role in the establishment of British domination over the Igbo people.

The first Christian missionaries to work in Igboland were agents of the Church Missionary Society (CMS), a branch of the Anglican Church. The CMS established a mission at Onitsha in 1857, and soon after in Alenso, Asaba, and other neighbouring towns. They subsequently opened more stations within a forty-mile radius of Onitsha and Asaba. The fiercest conflicts between the Igbo people and the

Igbo Christians

Europeans raged throughout that same region, conflicts that form the backdrop of Achebe's classic novel.

CMS missionaries were soon joined in the Onitsha and Asaba areas by two different Roman Catholic societies, the Holy Ghost Fathers and the priests of the Société des Missions Africaines (SMA). The Holy Ghost Fathers worked in Igboland east of the Niger River, while the SMA worked on the area west of the river. The CMS worked on both sides of the river. The three most memorable missionaries of that period were Reverend Samuel Ajayi Crowther of the CMS, Father Joseph Shanahan of the Holy Ghost Fathers, and Father Carlo Zappa of the SMA. It is interesting to note that many of the most effective CMS missionaries were in fact Africans. Rev. John Christopher Taylor was an Igbo man, born in Sierra Leone to freed slave parents. Rev. Crowther, later appointed bishop, was a former Yoruba slave. The Roman Catholics, on the other hand, relied entirely on European priests for their missionary work.

The Igbo had adopted a conciliatory stance in their early dealings with the missionaries, because the Igbo religion was pacific and the Igbo themselves respected the religious views of other people. The Igbo usually listened patiently to the Christians and then expected the missionaries to pay equal attention to their own viewpoints. Some Igbo saw the missionaries as essentially harmless, and shrugged at the uncomprehending priests who fraternized with outcasts and gainlessly occupied themselves with preaching.

Yet, if necessary, missionaries were prepared to destroy the entire system of Igbo customs and beliefs in order to convert the people to Christianity. Bishop Crowther himself saw Igbo society as evil, his ministry as a battle between light and darkness. Father Zappa criticized the 'foolishness' of following the religion of their forefathers. Father Shanahan described his mission as a battle against a 'baffling brick wall of failure'. Most missionaries painted ghastly pictures of Igbo society, which they sent back to Europe, and incited European governments and traders against the Igbo.

Missionaries expected British colonial agents to protect them, and, ignoring possible provocation, the British raided many Igbo towns on the grounds that they had harassed the missionaries. Some foreign missionaries actually provided strategic information about the villages where they worked for colonial armies on punitive expeditions. Encouraged by the British military presence, missionaries intensified their attack on Igbo customs. The new converts themselves became bolder and more intractable.

It took the Igbo a long while to realize that the missionaries were more dangerous than they appeared. In Obosi, the chiefs accosted Bishop Crowther and protested the tendency of the Christians to ignore the objects of worship of their forefathers, to kill and eat sacred snakes and fishes, and to pull down objects of worship and shrines. The chiefs demanded that Christian converts should confess the wrongs done to Igbo gods, pay for the damage, and promise not to repeat those wrongs in the future. In Alenso they murdered several Christians; in Illah and other villages to the south they burned down churches and drove the Christians away. Feeling cornered between missionary intransigence and a reckless imperial drive, the Igbo people fought back.

At this point, we can see a vicious cycle: the forces of the British Royal Company responded to these acts of violence with greater violence. The Royal Niger Company agreed to give official protection to Christians and to attack local communities who threatened them. Incited by missionary complaints that the people of Asaba still practiced human sacrifice, for example, Company forces raided Asaba in 1888 and destroyed half of it.

Despite their official backing, and their initial welcome, the first Christian missionaries made slow progress in Igboland. They had encountered a strong traditionalist society prepared to defend its customs.

The British Annexation of Igboland: The Era of Formal Empire

The actual British conquest of Igboland began in January 1900, following a growing intervention in Igbo affairs. The bombardments of Onitsha and Aboh in 1879 and 1883, respectively, had been authorized to protect British traders, and the destruction of half of Asaba in 1888 was intended to protect Christians. It was only in 1900 that the British imperial government declared Igboland a protectorate and embarked upon formal conquest.

Igbo Resistance to Colonial Rule: The Ekumeku Movement

Some Igbo communities rejected British annexation and backed this up by preparing for war. Even before colonial rule was imposed, many Western Igbo towns had suffered economic, military, and political decline as a result of the combined activities of British traders, imperial agents, and Christian missionaries. This may well explain why the earliest and the fiercest military clashes took place in Western Igboland. Many of these battles were fought under the umbrella of the Ekumeku movement.

Western Igbo communities launched the Ekumeku movement in 1898 to resist the disintegration of their society and to halt the advance of British imperialism. The Ekumeku wars were not a sudden outburst but the climax of a long period of political disturbances touched off by British cultural, commercial, and political ambitions on the Niger. Organized under the leadership of a union of titled chiefs, the movement achieved 'a far-flung coalition' against British military pressure. The Ekumeku warriors were young men, drawn from the town clubs and secret societies. They accepted silence and guerrilla tactics as their military strategies. Only men who took the oath of secrecy enrolled for service. Summoned through coded messages, they held their meetings in secret places. They selected several targets and attacked them simultaneously, creating panic among the European and Christian communities. They earned the nickname 'the Silent Ones' because of the unique way they silently carried out their activities. The Western Igbo resistance was finally crushed in 1914.

Resistance Movements East of the Niger River: The Aro Expedition

British operations in Eastern Igboland began in 1901. The best documented of these operations was the Aro expedition of 1901–02. The Aro were great traders and entrepreneurs, and had long met the needs of the hinterland peoples for imported European goods. They commanded widespread influence and respect among their neighbors, both because of their commercial expertise, and because of the role that the Aro oracle played in the judicial systems of the region. These economic interests motivated the Aro trading chiefs to unite several Igbo towns and to finance a war of resistance against Britain.

British activities in the Niger Delta and in the Cross River estuary had destroyed the communities with whom the Aro did business. For example, the Efik chiefs of the Cross River valley suffered a severe loss of trade and prestige as a result of the British intrusion. In the Niger Delta, British military forces destroyed Brass and treacherously kidnapped King Jaja of Opobo, exiling him to the West Indies. The vibrant commercial city-state of Opobo then entered a decline from which it never recovered. One finds a direct relationship between British incursions and the eclipse of the indigenous entrepreneurial classes in southeastern Nigeria. The British intention was to subordinate African business interests to European interests, as had happened during the era of the Atlantic slave trade; it was the refusal of Nigerian communities to accept that subordinate position that precipitated further military intervention.

Having defeated the Niger Delta and Cross River estuary communities, the British moved further inland to confront the Aro in 1901. They destroyed the Long Juju oracle and went on to punish neighboring Igbo communities. Somewhat surprisingly, it was neither the Aro nor the dreaded Abam warriors who put up the strongest resistance to the British. Other Igbo communities engaged the colonial forces in a running battle that lasted until after the First World War.

The Consolidation of British Rule in Igboland
British officials recognized that administering the Igbo people would be even more difficult than conquering them. The greatest challenge was how to rule the hundreds of Igbo towns and villages that recognized no centralized governments. In the Muslim parts of Northern Nigeria, by contrast, the British maintained much of the structure of the pre-existing Sokoto Caliphate; they simply reinforced the power and authority of the ruling classes of *emirs,* and then governed through them. But Igbo political structures were fragmented and small in scale; British officials could not comprehend the democratic genius of Igbo political organization, and felt more comfortable with the familiar hierarchies of kingdoms and empires.

Shortly after the British conquest of Igboland, officials moved to set up a system of African courts. Their aim was to replace indigenous institutions with a new structure of appointed officials called 'warrant chiefs' – so-called because their sole legitimacy derived from a colonial legal document, the warrant. These warrant chiefs and the British resident commissioners made bylaws and regulated local affairs. They controlled the local police and punished anyone who resisted colonial rule. These men were the tools with which the colonial government hoped to centralize the autonomous political institutions of the Igbo.

The system of warrant chiefs and native courts introduced dramatic changes into Igbo society. The laws that set them up brushed aside traditional judicial institutions. Cases that should have been decided by lineage and village elders – for example, Okonkwo's punishment for manslaughter in Achebe's novel – would now be tried by strangers. The district officers who controlled these native courts might have been trained in English law, but they had little or no knowledge of native laws and customs. As a result, many of their decisions contradicted Igbo ideas of justice.

The Igbo people protested against the warrant chief and native court systems, but their protests resulted only in punitive expeditions. The crisis came to a head in the late 1920s, when the British extended the principle of direct taxation into the 'untaxed provinces' of southern Nigeria. This policy sparked anti-tax riots in 1927–28, and the famous Aba women's riots of 1929. These widespread protests ultimately compelled the colonial administration to reorganize the native authority government in the 1930s and 1940s, leading to an improved system of native administration. British officials finally recognized that the poorly trained, and mostly illiterate, warrant chiefs, together with their small army of court clerks and messengers, could not be relied upon to collect taxes and discharge a host of administrative and judicial functions. Tied more closely to indigenous political institutions, the new administrative system remained operative until 1952, when it gave way to a regional government system that paved the way for constitutional reform and prepared Nigerians for political independence. In October 1960, the Igbo people joined other Nigerians in celebrating national independence.

Conclusions

The ancient Igbo communities were similar to other peoples who lived in the difficult environments of the premodern world. Their major preoccupations were to live free from crime and sickness, to live in harmony with unseen higher forces, to live in peace with themselves and their neighbors, to have many children and grandchildren, and to produce enough food. Some observers may argue that the Igbo methods were primitive, forgetting that the methods that other societies adopted were equally primitive. We must remember that the England, France, and Russia of today are totally different from the England, France, and Russia of five hundred years ago, just as Igboland of today is totally different from premodern Igboland. The careful reader should avoid making false comparisons between premodern African societies and modern European and American societies.

Still, it is quite striking how rapidly the Igbo people, despite their attachment to their customs, succumbed to European civilization. The fact that it took barely a hundred years (1857–1960) for the British to tear apart a society that had taken thousands of years to evolve suggests that European colonialism was a potent agent of change. Even more puzzling is the speed with which Christianity and Western education swept the Igbo people off their feet. In the long run, even those chiefs and community leaders who had organized and financed the wars of resistance converted to Christianity and helped the missionaries build schools and churches.

One explanation for this sudden rush to embrace Western civilization is that the Igbo were quick to perceive the importance of Western education in the new colonial structure. A second explanation is that the Igbo people were, and still are, often very eager to accept change. A third is that, as the ties that bound the communities disintegrated, the Igbo found new ones in Christianity and Western education. The result is that Igboland now has an unusually high concentration of Christian and Western-educated Africans. The Igbo seek membership in school and church organizations with as much enthusiasm as their forebears sought admission into the ancient age-groups, town clubs, and title associations. Barely a hundred years ago, Igbo people could hardly read or write. Today, Igbo professors occupy important faculty positions in universities in Africa, Europe, and America. Igbo medical practitioners work in hospitals around the globe, and their scientists, engineers, lawyers, and other professionals render useful services on every continent. Obviously the Igbo people have made material progress. It remains to be seen to what extent they will continue to barter their culture for material progress and be completely devoured by Western civilization.

Principal Characters in the Novel

Akuekue	daughter of Obierika, whose marriage is negotiated
Anene	Ekwefi's first husband
Chielo	the current priestess of the oracle
Chika	the former priestess of the oracle, during Unoka's time
Ekwefi	Okonkwo's second wife; mother of Ezinma
Enoch	a Christian convert; a fanatic, who killed the sacred python and sought confrontation with Igbo traditionalists
Ezeani	the priest of the earth goddess
Ezeudu	an important elder; the oldest man in Okonkwo's village
Ezeugo	a powerful orator usually chosen as spokesman
Ezinma	Okonkwo's favorite daughter
Ikemefuna	the boy from Mbaino given to Umuofia as compensation for murder
Maduka	son of Obierika, a promising young wrestler
Mr. Brown	the first white missionary based in Umuofia
Mr. Kiaga	the Igbo missionary left in charge of the fledgling church in Mbanta
Mr. Smith	the zealous white missionary who replaced Mr. Brown
Ndulue	husband who died at the same time as his wife
Nwakibie	a big man in Umuofia, who helped Okonkwo get started in planting yams
Nwoye	Okonkwo's oldest son, who converts to Christianity and adopts the name Isaac
Obiageli	sister of Nwoye
Obierika	Okonkwo's good friend and confidant

Ogbuefi Udo	the man whose wife was murdered by the people of Mbaino
Ojiugo	one of Okonkwo's three wives, mother of Obiageli
Okagbue	the medicine man who finds and destroys Ezinma's *iyi-uwa*
Okonkwo	the main character, a strong, proud man
Okoye	a friend of Okonkwo's father, who tries unsuccessfully to get back the money Unoka had borrowed
Ozoemena	wife who dies at the same time as her husband
Uchendu	Okonkwo's uncle, the senior man of Mbanta where Okonkwo's family lives in exile
Unoka	Okonkwo's late father, an easygoing, rather lazy person

Glossary of Words and Phrases Used in the Text

(Igbo terms are in italics; *o* indicates 'aw' sound as in awful)

Afo	one of the four market days
agadi-nwayi	old woman
agbala	woman; also, an insulting term for a man who has taken no title
Agbala	the name of the oracle consulted by the people of Umuofia
Amadioha	the god of thunder and lightning
Ani	the earth goddess
bride-price	or bridewealth; the gifts transferred from the groom's family to that of the bride, which cement the marriage and legitimize the children
chi	one's personal god, or guardian spirit
Chukwu	the supreme god
cowries	shells imported from the Indian Ocean, widely used as currency in precolonial Africa
District Commissioner	the British official in charge of a particular African district
efulefu	an empty, worthless man
egwugwu	the masked spirits, representing the ancestral spirits of the village
Eke	one of the four market days
ekwe	a wooden drum
eneke-nti-oba	a kind of bird
eze-agai-nwayi	the teeth of an old woman
foo-foo	(or fufu) pounded yam eaten as part of most meals
harmattan	a cold, dry wind that blows from the North
iba	fever

liii

Ibo	the older spelling of 'Igbo,' less commonly used today
Idemile	one of the three most prestigious titles in Igboland
Ifejioku	the god of yams, the men's crop and principal food of the Igbo
Iguedo	Okonkwo's village, one of the nine villages that make up Umuofia
ikenga	a wooden carving that becomes imbued with a man's personal spirit
ilo	the village common, where meetings, ceremonies, and sports competitions take place
inyanga	showing off; bragging
isa-ifi	a ceremony held to determine faithfulness if a woman had been separated from her fiancé or husband for some time and were then reunited with him
iyi-uwa	a special stone that forms the link between an *ogbanje* and the spirit world. The child would eventually die if the *iyi-uwa* were not discovered and destroyed.
jigida	a string of waist beads
kite	a bird that appears during the dry season
kola nuts	offered to guests on special occasions
kotma	'court man', or court messenger; a corruption of the English term
kwenu	a shout of approval and greeting
maize	corn
ndichie	the elders, who meet in council and make decisions binding the clan
nna ayi	our father
nne	mother
nno	an expression of welcome
nso-ani	sacrilege
nza	a tiny bird
obi	the living quarters of the head of the family
obodo dike	the land of the brave
ochu	murder or manslaughter

ogbanje	a changeling; a child who repeatedly dies and returns to its mother to be reborn
Ogbuefi	an honorific used before the name of a man who has taken the *ozo* title
ogene	a kind of gong
ogwu	supernatural medicine
osu	an outcast; having been dedicated to a god, the *osu* was not allowed to mix with the freeborn, or to marry one of them
Oye	one of the four market days
ozo	one of the titles an important Igbo man could aspire to
palm kernels	the core of the fruit of the oil palm tree, which were cracked to release the oil
palm oil	used in cooking and for preparing food, also a major cash crop exported to Europe
palm wine	a fermented drink prepared from the sap of certain palm trees
plantain	a starchy kind of banana, cooked as food
pottage	a stew
singlets	men's undershirts
sisal	a kind of cactus plant with fibrous leaves
tufia	a curse or oath
udu	a type of drum made from pottery
uli	a dye used by women for drawing patterns on the skin
umuada	a family gathering of daughters, for which the female kinsfolk return to their village of origin
Umuofia	the clan Okonkwo belonged to, made up of nine villages
umunna	a wide group of kinsmen (the masculine form of *umuada*)
Uri	part of the betrothal ceremony when the dowry or bridewealth is paid

Suggestions for Further Reading

I. About Chinua Achebe and His Writing

Carroll, David. *Chinua Achebe*. 2nd ed. New York: St. Martin's, 1980.

Gikandi, Simon. *Reading Chinua Achebe: Language and Ideology in Fiction*. London: Heinemann, 1991.

Innes, C. L. *Chinua Achebe*. Cambridge: Cambridge University Press, 1990.

Innes, C. L., and Lindfors, Bernth, eds., *Critical Perspectives on Chinua Achebe*. Washington, D.C.: Three Continents Press, 1978.

Killam, G. D. *The Writings of Chinua Achebe*. London: Heinemann, 1969; revised 1977.

Lindfors, Bernth, ed. *Approaches to Teaching Achebe's Things Fall Apart*. New York: Modern Language Association, 1991.

Rutherford, A., and Peterson, K. H. eds. *Chinua Achebe: A Celebration*. London: Heinemann, 1991.

Wren, Robert M. *Achebe's World: The Historical and Cultural Context of the Novels*. Washington, D.C.: Three Continents Press, 1980.

II. About Igbo Society and History

Afigbo, Adiele E. *The Warrant Chiefs: Indirect Rule in Southeastern Nigeria 1891–1929*. London: Longman, 1972.

Afigbo, Adiele E. *Ropes of Sand: Studies in Igbo History and Culture*. Ibadan: Oxford University Press, 1981.

Amadiume, Ifi. *Male Daughters, Female Husbands: Gender and Sex in an African Society*. London: Zed Books, 1987.

Anene, J. C. *Southern Nigeria in Transition, 1885–1906*. Cambridge: Cambridge University Press, 1966.

Basden, George T. *Niger Ibos* [1938]. London: Frank Cass, 1966.

Ekechi, Felix N. *Missionary Enterprise and Rivalry in Igboland 1857–1914*. London: Frank Cass, 1971.

Green, M. M. *Ibo Village Affairs, Chiefly with Reference to the Village of Umueke Agbaja*. London: Frank Cass, 1964.

Henderson, Richard N. *The King in Every Man: Evolutionary Trends in Onitsha-Ibo Society and Culture*. New Haven: Yale University Press, 1972.

Isichei, Elizabeth *A History of the Igbo People*. London: Macmillan, 1976.

Leith-Ross, Sylvia. *African Women: A Study of the Ibo of Nigeria* [1939]. London: Routledge, 1965.

Martin, Susan M. *Palm Oil and Protest: An Economic History of the Ngwa Region, Southeastern Nigeria, 1800–1980*. Cambridge: Cambridge University Press, 1988.

Ohadike, Don C. *The Ekumeku Movement: Western Igbo Resistance to the British Conquest of Nigeria, 1883–1914*. Athens, Ohio: Ohio University Press, 1991.

Onwuejeogwu, Michael A. *An Igbo Civilization: Nri Kingdom and Hegemony*. London: Ethnographica, 1981.

Ottenberg, Simon. *Leadership and Authority in an African Society: Afikpo Village-Group*. Seattle: University of Washington Press, 1971.

Thomas, Northcote W. *Anthropological Report on the Ibo-Speaking People of Nigeria*. London: Harrison, 1913–1914.

Uchendu, Victor C. *The Igbo of Southeast Nigeria*. New York: Holt, Rinehart and Winston, 1965.

III. The Principal Works of Chinua Achebe

Things Fall Apart. London: Heinemann, 1958.

No Longer at Ease. London: Heinemann, 1960.

The Sacrificial Egg and Other Short Stories. Onitsha: Etudo Ltd, 1962.

Arrow of God. London: Heinemann, 1964.

A Man of the People. London: Heinemann, 1966.

Beware Soul Brother and Other Poems. London: Heinemann, 1972; reprinted by Anchor/Doubleday as *Christmas in Biafra and Other Poems* (New York, 1973).

(Ed.) *The Insider: Stories of War and Peace from Nigeria.* Enugu: Nwankwo-Ifejika, 1971.

Girls at War and Other Stories. London: Heinemann, 1972; Garden City, NY: Anchor/Doubleday, 1973.

Morning Yet on Creation Day: Essays. London: Heinemann, 1975; Garden City, NY: Anchor/Doubleday, 1975.

The Trouble with Nigeria [Essays]. London: Heinemann, 1983.

Anthills of the Savanna. London: Heinemann, 1987; Garden City, NY: Anchor/Doubleday, 1988.

IV. Other Classic Novels About Igbo Society

Amadi, Elechi. *The Concubine.* London: Heinemann, 1966.

Amadi, Elechi. *The Great Ponds.* London: Heinemann, 1969.

Amadi, Elechi. *The Slave.* London: Heinemann, 1978.

Ekwensi, Cyprian. *Jagua Nana* [1961]. London: Heinemann, 1975.

Ekwensi, Cyprian. *People of the City* [1954]. London: Heinemann, 1963.

Emecheta, Buchi. *Destination Biafra* [1982]. London: Heinemann, 1994.

Emecheta, Buchi. *The Joys of Motherhood* [1979]. London: Heinemann, 1994.

Emecheta, Buchi. *Kehinde.* London: Heinemann, 1994.

Nwapa, Flora. *Efuru.* London: Heinemann, 1966.

Nwapa, Flora. *Idu.* London: Heinemann, 1970.

THINGS FALL APART

Turning and turning in the widening gyre
The falcon cannot hear the falconer;
Things fall apart; the centre cannot hold;
Mere anarchy is loosed upon the world.

W. B. Yeats, 'The Second Coming'

PART ONE

Chapter One

Okonkwo was well known throughout the nine villages and even beyond. His fame rested on solid personal achievements. As a young man of eighteen he had brought honour to his village by throwing Amalinze the Cat. Amalinze was the great wrestler who for seven years was unbeaten, from Umuofia to Mbaino. He was called the Cat because his back would never touch the earth. It was this man that Okonkwo threw in a fight which the old men agreed was one of the fiercest since the founder of their town engaged a spirit of the wild for seven days and seven nights.

The drums beat and the flutes sang and the spectators held their breath. Amalinze was a wily craftsman, but Okonkwo was as slippery as a fish in water. Every nerve and every muscle stood out on their arms, on their backs and their thighs, and one almost heard them stretching to breaking point. In the end Okonkwo threw the Cat.

That was many years ago, twenty years or more, and during this time Okonkwo's fame had grown like a bush-fire in the harmattan. He was tall and huge, and his bushy eyebrows and wide nose gave him a very severe look. He breathed heavily, and it was said that, when he slept, his wives and children in their out-houses could hear him breathe. When he walked, his heels hardly touched the ground and he seemed to walk on springs, as if he was going to pounce on somebody. And he did pounce on people quite often. He had a slight stammer and whenever he was angry and could not get his words out quickly enough, he would use his fists. He had no patience with unsuccessful men. He had had no patience with his father.

Unoka, for that was his father's name, had died ten years ago. In his day he was lazy and improvident and was quite incapable of thinking about tomorrow. If any money came his way, and it seldom did, he immediately bought gourds of palm-wine, called round his neighbours and made merry. He always said that whenever he saw a dead man's mouth he saw the folly of not eating what one had in one's lifetime. Unoka was, of course, a debtor, and he owed every neighbour some money, from a few cowries to quite substantial amounts.

He was tall but very thin and had a slight stoop. He wore a haggard and mournful look except when he was drinking or playing on his flute. He was very good on his flute, and his happiest moments were the two or three moons after the harvest when the village musicians brought down their instruments, hung above the fireplace. Unoka would play with them, his face beaming with blessedness and peace. Sometimes another village would ask Unoka's band and their dancing *egwugwu* to come and stay with them and teach them their tunes. They would go to such hosts for as long as three or four markets, making music and feasting. Unoka loved the good fare and the good fellowship, and he loved this season of the year, when the rains had stopped and the sun rose every morning with dazzling beauty. And it was not too hot either, because the cold and dry harmattan wind was blowing down from the north. Some years the harmattan was very severe and a dense haze hung on the atmosphere. Old men and children would then sit round log fires, warming their bodies. Unoka loved it all, and he loved the first kites that returned with the dry season, and the children who sang songs of welcome to them. He would remember his own childhood, how he had often wandered around looking for a kite sailing leisurely against the blue sky. As soon as he found one he would sing with his whole being, welcoming it back from its long, long journey, and asking it if it had brought home any lengths of cloth.

That was years ago, when he was young. Unoka, the grown-up, was a failure. He was poor and his wife and children had barely enough to eat. People laughed at him because he was a loafer, and they swore never to lend him any more money because he never paid back. But Unoka was such a man that he always succeeded in borrowing more, and piling up his debts.

One day a neighbour called Okoye came in to see him. He was reclining on a mud bed in his hut playing on the flute. He immediately rose and shook hands with Okoye, who then unrolled the goatskin

4

which he carried under his arm, and sat down. Unoka went into an inner room and soon returned with a small wooden disc containing a kola nut, some alligator pepper and a lump of white chalk.

'I have kola,' he announced when he sat down, and passed the disc over to his guest.

'Thank you. He who brings kola brings life. But i think you ought to break it,' replied Okoye passing back the disc.

'No, it is for you, I think,' and they argued like this for a few moments before Unoka accepted the honour of breaking the kola. Okoye, meanwhile, took the lump of chalk, drew some lines on the floor, and then painted his big toe. As he broke the kola, Unoka prayed to their ancestors for life and health, and for protection against their enemies. When they had eaten they talked about many things: about the heavy rains which were drowning the yams, about the next ancestral feast and about the impending war with the village of Mbaino. Unoka was never happy when it came to wars. He was in fact a coward and could not bear the sight of blood. And so he changed the subject and talked about music, and his face beamed. He could hear in his mind's ear the blood-stirring and intricate rhythms of the *ekwe* and the *udu* and the *ogene*, and he could hear his own flute weaving in and out of them, decorating them with a colourful and plaintive tune. The total effect was gay and brisk, but if one picked out the flute as it went up and down and then broke up into short snatches, one saw that there was sorrow and grief there.

Okoye was also a musician. He played on the *ogene*. But he was not a failure like Unoka. He had a large barn full of yams and he had three wives. And now he was going to take the Idemili title, the third highest in the land. It was a very expensive ceremony and he was gathering all his resources together. That was in fact the reason why he had come to see Unoka. He cleared his throat and began:

'Thank you for the kola. You may have heard of the title I intend to take shortly.'

Having spoken plainly so far, Okoye said the next half a dozen sentences in proverbs. Among the Ibo the art of conversation is regarded very highly, and proverbs are the palm-oil with which words are eaten. Okoye was a great talker and he spoke for a long time, skirting round the subject and then hitting it finally. In short, he was

5

asking Unoka to return the two hundred cowries he had borrowed from him more than two years before. As soon as Unoka understood what his friend was driving at, he burst out laughing. He laughed loud and long and his voice rang out clear as the *ogene*, and tears stood in his eyes. His visitor was amazed, and sat speechless. At the end, Unoka was able to give an answer between fresh outbursts of mirth.

'Look at that wall,' he said, pointing at the far wall of his hut, which was rubbed with red earth so that it shone. 'Look at those lines of chalk;' and Okoye saw groups of short perpendicular lines drawn in chalk. There were five groups, and the smallest group had ten lines. Unoka had a sense of the dramatic and so he allowed a pause, in which he took a pinch of snuff and sneezed noisily, and then he continued: 'Each group there represents a debt to someone, and each stroke is one hundred cowries. You see, I owe that man a thousand cowries. But he has not come to wake me up in the morning for it. I shall pay you, but not today. Our elders say that the sun will shine on those who stand before it shines on those who kneel under them. I shall pay my big debts first.' And he took another pinch of snuff, as if that was paying the big debts first. Okoye rolled his goatskin and departed.

When Unoka died he had taken no title at all and he was heavily in debt. Any wonder then that his son Okonkwo was ashamed of him? Fortunately, among these people a man was judged according to his worth and not according to the worth of his father. Okonkwo was clearly cut out for great things. He was still young but he had won fame as the greatest wrestler in the nine villages. He was a wealthy farmer and had two barns full of yams, and had just married his third wife. To crown it all he had taken two titles and had shown incredible prowess in two inter-tribal wars. And so although Okonkwo was still young, he was already one of the greatest men of his time. Age was respected among his people, but achievement was revered. As the elders said, if a child washed his hands he could eat with kings. Okonkwo had clearly washed his hands and so he ate with kings and elders. And that was how he came to look after the doomed lad who was sacrificed to the village of Umuofia by their neighbours to avoid war and bloodshed. The ill-fated lad was called Ikemefuna.

Chapter Two

Okonkwo had just blown out the palm-oil lamp and stretched himself on his bamboo bed when he heard the *ogene* of the town-crier piercing the still night air. *Gome, gome, gome, gome*, boomed the hollow metal. Then the crier gave his message, and at the end of it beat his instrument again. And this was the message. Every man of Umuofia was asked to gather at the market-place tomorrow morning. Okonkwo wondered what was amiss, for he knew certainly that something was amiss. He had discerned a clear overtone of tragedy in the crier's voice, and even now he could still hear it as it grew dimmer and dimmer in the distance.

The night was very quiet. It was always quiet except on moonlight nights. Darkness held a vague terror for these people, even the bravest among them. Children were warned not to whistle at night for fear of evil spirits. Dangerous animals became even more sinister and uncanny in the dark. A snake was never called by its name at night, because it would hear. It was called a string. And so on this particular night as the crier's voice was gradually swallowed up in the distance, silence returned to the world, a vibrant silence made more intense by the universal trill of a million million forest insects.

On a moonlight night it would be different. The happy voices of children playing in open fields would then be heard. And perhaps those not so young would be playing in pairs in less open places, and old men and women would remember their youth. As the Ibo say: 'When the moon is shining the cripple becomes hungry for a walk.'

But this particular night was dark and silent. And in all the nine villages of Umuofia a town-crier with his *ogene* asked every man to be present tomorrow morning. Okonkwo on his bamboo bed tried to figure out the nature of the emergency – war with a neighbouring clan? That seemed the most likely reason, and he was not afraid of war. He was a man of action, a man of war. Unlike his father he could stand the look of blood. In Umuofia's latest war he was the first to bring home a human head. That was his fifth head; and he was not an old man yet. On great occasions such as the funeral of a village celebrity he drank his palm-wine from his first human head.

In the morning the market-place was full. There must have been about ten thousand men there, all talking in low voices. At last Ogbuefi Ezeugo stood up in the midst of them and bellowed four times, 'Umuofia kwenu,' and on each occasion he faced a different direction and seemed to push the air with a clenched fist. And ten thousand men answered 'Yaa!' each time. Then there was perfect silence. Ogbuefi Ezeugo was a powerful orator and was always chosen to speak on such occasions. He moved his hand over his white head and stroked his white beard. He then adjusted his cloth, which was passed under his right arm-pit and tied above his left shoulder.

'Umuofia kwenu,' he bellowed a fifth time, and the crowd yelled in answer. And then suddenly like one possessed he shot out his left hand and pointed in the direction of Mbaino, and said through gleaming white teeth firmly clenched: 'Those sons of wild animals have dared to murder a daughter of Umuofia.' He threw his head down and gnashed his teeth, and allowed a murmur of suppressed anger to sweep the crowd. When he began again, the anger on his face was gone and in its place a sort of smile hovered, more terrible and more sinister than the anger. And in a clear unemotional voice he told Umuofia how their daughter had gone to market at Mbaino and had been killed. That woman, said Ezeugo, was the wife of Ogbuefi Udo, and he pointed to a man who sat near him with a bowed head. The crowd then shouted with anger and thirst for blood.

Many others spoke, and at the end it was decided to follow the normal course of action. An ultimatum was immediately dispatched to Mbaino asking them to choose between war on the one hand, and on the other the offer of a young man and a virgin as compensation.

Umuofia was feared by all its neighbours. It was powerful in war and in magic, and its priests and medicine-men were feared in all the surrounding country. Its most potent war-medicine was as old as the clan itself. Nobody knew how old. But on one point there was general agreement – the active principle in that medicine had been an old woman with one leg. In fact, the medicine itself was called *agadi-nwayi*, or old woman. It had its shrine in the centre of Umuofia, in a cleared spot. And if anybody was so foolhardy as to pass by the shrine after dusk he was sure to see the old woman hopping about.

And so the neighbouring clans who naturally knew of these things feared Umuofia, and would not go to war against it without first trying a peaceful settlement. And in fairness to Umuofia it should be recorded that it never went to war unless its case was clear and just and was accepted as such by its Oracle – the Oracle of the Hills and the Caves. And there were indeed occasions when the Oracle had forbidden Umuofia to wage a war. If the clan had disobeyed the Oracle they would surely have been beaten, because their dreaded *agadi-nwayi* would never fight what the Ibo call *a fight of blame*.

But the war that now threatened was a just war. Even the enemy clan knew that. And so when Okonkwo of Umuofia arrived at Mbaino as the proud and imperious emissary of war, he was treated with great honour and respect, and two days later he returned home with a lad of fifteen and a young virgin. The lad's name was Ikemefuna, whose sad story is still told in Umuofia unto this day.

The elders, or *ndichie*, met to hear a report of Okonkwo's mission. At the end they decided, as everybody knew they would, that the girl should go to Ogbuefi Udo to replace his murdered wife. As for the boy, he belonged to the clan as a whole, and there was no hurry to decide his fate. Okonkwo was, therefore, asked on behalf of the clan to look after him in the interim. And so for three years Ikemefuna lived in Okonkwo's household.

◆

Okonkwo ruled his household with a heavy hand. His wives, especially the youngest, lived in perpetual fear of his fiery temper, and so did his little children. Perhaps down in his heart Okonkwo was not a cruel man. But his whole life was dominated by fear, the fear of failure and of weakness. It was deeper and more intimate than the fear of evil and capricious gods and of magic, the fear of the forest, and the forces of nature, malevolent, red in tooth and claw. Okonkwo's fear was greater than these. It was not external but lay deep

9

within himself. It was the fear of himself, lest he should be found to resemble his father. Even as a little boy he had resented his father's failure and weakness, and even now he still remembered how he had suffered when a playmate had told him that his father was *agbala*. That was how Okonkwo first came to know that *agbala* was not only another name for a woman, it could also mean a man who had taken no title. And so Okonkwo was ruled by one passion – to hate everything that his father Unoka had loved. One of those things was gentleness and another was idleness.

During the planting season Okonkwo worked daily on his farms from cock-crow until the chickens went to roost. He was a very strong man and rarely felt fatigue. But his wives and young children were not as strong, and so they suffered. But they dared not complain openly. Okonkwo's first son, Nwoye, was then twelve years old but was already causing his father great anxiety for his incipient laziness. At any rate, that was how it looked to his father, and he sought to correct him by constant nagging and beating. And so Nwoye was developing into a sad-faced youth.

Okonkwo's prosperity was visible in his household. He had a large compound enclosed by a thick wall of red earth. His own hut, or *obi*, stood immediately behind the only gate in the red walls. Each of his three wives had her own hut, which together formed a half moon behind the *obi*. The barn was built against one end of the red walls, and long stacks of yam stood out prosperously in it. At the opposite end of the compound was a shed for the goats, and each wife built a small attachment to her hut for the hens. Near the barn was a small house, the 'medicine house' or shrine where Okonkwo kept the wooden symbols of his personal god and of his ancestral spirits. He worshipped them with sacrifices of kola nut, food and palm-wine, and offered prayers to them on behalf of himself, his three wives and eight children.

◆

So when the daughter of Umuofia was killed in Mbaino, Ikemefuna came into Okonkwo's household. When Okonkwo brought him home that day he called his most senior wife and handed him over to her.

'He belongs to the clan,' he told her. 'So look after him.'

'Is he staying long with us?' she asked.

'Do what you are told, woman,' Okonkwo thundered, and stammered. 'When did you become one of the *ndichie* of Umuofia?'

And so Nwoye's mother took Ikemefuna to her hut and asked no more questions.

As for the boy himself, he was terribly afraid. He could not understand what was happening to him or what he had done. How could he know that his father had taken a hand in killing a daughter of Umuofia? All he knew was that a few men had arrived at their house, conversing with his father in low tones, and at the end he had been taken out and handed over to a stranger. His mother had wept bitterly, but he had been too surprised to weep. And so the stranger had brought him, and a girl, a long, long way from home, through lonely forest paths. He did not know who the girl was, and he never saw her again.

Chapter Three

Okonkwo did not have the start in life which many young men usually had. He did not inherit a barn from his father. There was no barn to inherit. The story was told in Umuofia of how his father, Unoka, had gone to consult the Oracle of the Hills and the Caves to find out why he always had a miserable harvest.

The Oracle was called Agbala, and people came from far and near to consult it. They came when misfortune dogged their steps or when they had a dispute with their neighbours. They came to discover what the future held for them or to consult the spirits of their departed fathers.

The way into the shrine was a round hole at the side of a hill, just a little bigger than the round opening into a hen-house. Worshippers and those who came to seek knowledge from the god crawled on their belly through the hole and found themselves in a dark, endless space in the presence of Agbala. No one had ever beheld Agbala, except his priestess. But no one who had ever crawled into his awful shrine had come out without the fear of his power. His priestess stood by the sacred fire which she built in the heart of the cave and proclaimed the will of the god. The fire did not burn with a flame. The glowing logs only served to light up vaguely the dark figure of the priestess.

Sometimes a man came to consult the spirit of his dead father or relative. It was said that when such a spirit appeared, the man saw it vaguely in the darkness, but never heard its voice. Some people even said that they had heard the spirits flying and flapping their wings against the roof of the cave.

Many years ago when Okonkwo was still a boy his father, Unoka, had gone to consult Agbala. The priestess in those days was a woman called Chika. She was full of the power of her god, and she was greatly feared. Unoka stood before her and began his story.

'Every year,' he said sadly, 'before I put any crop in the earth, I

12

sacrifice a cock to Ani, the owner of all land. It is the law of our fathers. I also kill a cock at the shrine of Ifejioku, the god of yams. I clear the bush and set fire to it when it is dry. I sow the yams when the first rain has fallen, and stake them when the young tendrils appear. I weed – '

'Hold your peace!' screamed the priestess, her voice terrible as it echoed through the dark void. 'You have offended neither the gods nor your fathers. And when a man is at peace with his gods and his ancestors, his harvest will be good or bad according to the strength of his arm. You, Unoka, are known in all the clan for the weakness of your matchet and your hoe. When your neighbours go out with their axe to cut down virgin forests, you sow your yams on exhausted farms that take no labour to clear. They cross seven rivers to make their farms; you stay at home and offer sacrifices to a reluctant soil. Go home and work like a man.'

Unoka was an ill-fated man. He had a bad *chi* or personal god, and evil fortune followed him to the grave, or rather to his death, for he had no grave. He died of the swelling which was an abomination to the earth goddess. When a man was afflicted with swelling in the stomach and the limbs he was not allowed to die in the house. He was carried to the Evil Forest and left there to die. There was a story of a very stubborn man who staggered back to his house and had to be carried again to the forest and tied to a tree. The sickness was an abomination to the earth, and so the victim could not be buried in her bowels. He died and rotted away above the earth, and was not given the first or the second burial. Such was Unoka's fate. When they carried him away, he took with him his flute.

With a father like Unoka, Okonkwo did not have the start in life which many young men had. He neither inherited a barn nor a title, nor even a young wife. But in spite of these disadvantages, he had begun even in his father's lifetime to lay the foundations of a prosperous future. It was slow and painful. But he threw himself into it like one possessed. And indeed he was possessed by the fear of his father's contemptible life and shameful death.

◆

There was a wealthy man in Okonkwo's village who had three huge barns, nine wives and thirty children. His name was Nwakibie and he had taken the highest but one title which a man could take in the clan. It was for this man that Okonkwo worked to earn his first seed yams.

He took a pot of palm-wine and a cock of Nwakibie. Two elderly neighbours were sent for, and Nwakibie's two grown-up sons were also present in his *obi*. He presented a kola nut and an alligator pepper, which was passed round for all to see and then returned to him. He broke it, saying: 'We shall all live. We pray for life, children, a good harvest and happiness. You will have what is good for you and I will have what is good for me. Let the kite perch and let the eagle perch too. If one says no to the other, let his wing break.'

After the kola nut had been eaten Okonkwo brought his palm-wine from the corner of the hut where it had been placed and stood it in the centre of the group. He addressed Nwakibie, calling him 'Our father'.

'*Nna ayi*,' he said. 'I have brought you this little kola. As our people say, a man who pays respect to the great paves the way for his own greatness. I have come to pay you my respects and also to ask a favour. But let us drink the wine first.'

Everybody thanked Okonkwo and the neighbours brought out their drinking horns from the goatskin bags they carried. Nwakibie brought down his own horn, which was fastened to the rafters. The younger of his sons, who was also the youngest man in the group, moved to the centre, raised the pot on his left knee and began to pour out the wine. The first cup went to Okonkwo, who must taste his wine before anyone else. Then the group drank, beginning with the eldest man. When everyone had drunk two or three horns, Nwakibie sent for his wives. Some of them were not at home and only four came in.

'Is Anasi not in?' he asked them. They said she was coming. Anasi was the first wife and the others could not drink before her, and so they stood waiting.

Anasi was a middle-aged woman, tall and strongly built. There was authority in her bearing and she looked every inch the ruler of the womenfolk in a large and prosperous family. She wore the anklet of her husband's titles, which the first wife alone could wear.

She walked up to her husband and accepted the horn from him. She then went down on one knee, drank a little and handed back the horn. She rose, called him by his name and went back to her hut. The other wives drank in the same way, in their proper order, and went away.

The men then continued their drinking and talking. Ogbuefi Idigo was talking about the palm-wine tapper, Obiako, who suddenly gave up his trade.

'There must be something behind it,' he said, wiping the foam of wine from his moustache with the back of his left hand. 'There must be a reason for it. A toad does not run in the daytime for nothing.'

'Some people say the Oracle warned him that he would fall off a palm tree and kill himself,' said Akukalia.

'Obiako has always been a strange one,' said Nwakibie. 'I have heard that many years ago, when his father had not been dead very long, he had gone to consult the Oracle. The Oracle said to him, "Your dead father wants you to sacrifice a goat to him." Do you know what he told the Oracle? He said, "Ask my dead father if he ever had a fowl when he was alive."' Everybody laughed heartily except Okonkwo, who laughed uneasily because as the saying goes, an old woman is always uneasy when dry bones are mentioned in a proverb. Okonkwo remembered his own father.

At last the young man who was pouring out the wine held up half a horn of the thick, white dregs and said, 'What we are eating is finished.' 'We have seen it,' the others replied. 'Who will drink the dregs?' he asked. 'Whoever has a job in hand,' said Idigo, looking at Nwakibie's elder son, Igwelo, with a mischievous twinkle in his eye.

Everybody agreed that Igwelo should drink the dregs. He accepted the half-full horn from his brother and drank it. As Idigo had said, Igwelo had a job in hand because he had married his first wife a month or two before. The thick dregs of palm-wine were supposed to be good for men who were going in to their wives.

After the wine had been drunk Okonkwo laid his difficulties before Nwakibie.

'I have come to you for help,' he said. 'Perhaps you can already guess what it is. I have cleared a farm but have no yams to sow. I know what it is to ask a man to trust another with his yams, especially these days when young men are afraid of hard work. I am not afraid

15

of work. The lizard that jumped from the high iroko tree to the ground said he would praise himself if no one else did. I began to fend for myself at an age when most people still suck at their mothers' breasts. If you give me some yam seeds I shall not fail you.'

Nwakibie cleared his throat. 'It pleases me to see a young man like you these days when our youth have gone so soft. Many young men have come to me to ask for yams but I have refused because I knew they would just dump them in the earth and leave them to be choked by weeds. When I say no to them they think I am hard-hearted. But it is not so. Eneke the bird says that since men have learnt to shoot without missing, he has learnt to fly without perching. I have learnt to be stingy with my yams. But I can trust you. I know it as I look at you. As our fathers said, you can tell a ripe corn by its look. I shall give you twice four hundred yams. Go ahead and prepare your farm.'

Okonkwo thanked him again and again and went home feeling happy. He knew that Nwakibie would not refuse him, but he had not expected he would be so generous. He had not hoped to get more than four hundred seeds. He would now have to make a bigger farm. He hoped to get another four hundred yams from one of his father's friends at Isiuzo.

Share-cropping was a very slow way of building up a barn of one's own. After all the toil one only got a third of the harvest. But for a young man whose father had no yams, there was no other way. And what made it worse in Okonkwo's case was that he had to support his mother and two sisters from his meagre harvest. And supporting his mother also meant supporting his father. She could not be expected to cook and eat while her husband starved. And so at a very early age when he was striving desperately to build a barn through share-cropping Okonkwo was also fending for his father's house. It was like pouring grains of corn into a bag full of holes. His mother and sisters worked hard enough, but they grew women's crops, like coco-yams, beans and cassava. Yam, the king of crops, was a man's crop.

◆

The year that Okonkwo took eight hundred seed-yams from Nwakibie was the worst year in living memory. Nothing happened at its proper

16

time; it was either too early or too late. It seemed as if the world had gone mad. The first rains were late, and, when they came, lasted only a brief moment. The blazing sun returned, more fierce than it had ever been known, and scorched all the green that had appeared with the rains. The earth burned like hot coals and roasted all the yams that had been sown. Like all good farmers, Okonkwo had begun to sow with the first rains. He had sown four hundred seeds when the rains dried up and the heat returned. He watched the sky all day for signs of rain-clouds and lay awake all night. In the morning he went back to his farm and saw the withering tendrils. He had tried to protect them from the smouldering earth by making rings of thick sisal leaves around them. But by the end of the day the sisal rings were burnt dry and grey. He changed them every day, and prayed that the rain might fall in the night. But the drought continued for eight market weeks and the yams were killed.

Some farmers had not planted their yams yet. They were the lazy easy-going ones who always put off clearing their farms as long as they could. This year they were the wise ones. They sympathised with their neighbours with much shaking of the head, but inwardly they were happy for what they took to be their own foresight.

Okonkwo planted what was left of his seed-yams when the rains finally returned. He had one consolation. The yams he had sown before the drought were his own, the harvest of the previous year. He still had the eight hundred from Nwakibie and the four hundred from his father's friend. So he would make a fresh start.

But the year had gone mad. Rain fell as it had never fallen before. For days and nights together it poured down in violent torrents, and washed away the yam heaps. Trees were uprooted and deep gorges appeared everywhere. Then the rain became less violent. But it went on from day to day without a pause. The spell of sunshine which always came in the middle of the wet season did not appear. The yams put on luxuriant green leaves, but every farmer knew that without sunshine the tubers would not grow.

That year the harvest was sad, like a funeral, and many farmers wept as they dug up the miserable and rotting yams. One man tied his cloth to a tree branch and hanged himself.

Okonkwo remembered that tragic year with a cold shiver throughout the rest of his life. It always surprised him when he thought of it later that he did not sink under the load of despair. He knew he was a fierce fighter, but that year had been enough to break the heart of a lion.

'Since I survived that year,' he always said, 'I shall survive anything.' He put it down to his inflexible will.

His father, Unoka, who was then an ailing man, had said to him during that terrible harvest month: 'Do not despair. I know you will not despair. You have a manly and a proud heart. A proud heart can survive a general failure because such a failure does not prick its pride. It is more difficult and more bitter when a man fails *alone*.'

Unoka was like that in his last days. His love of talk had grown with age and sickness. It tried Okonkwo's patience beyond words.

Chapter Four

'Looking at a king's mouth,' said an old man, 'one would think he never sucked at his mother's breast.' He was talking about Okonkwo, who had risen so suddenly from great poverty and misfortune to be one of the lords of the clan. The old man bore no ill-will towards Okonkwo. Indeed he respected him for his industry and success. But he was struck, as most people were, by Okonkwo's brusqueness in dealing with less successful men. Only a week ago a man had contradicted him at a kindred meeting which they held to discuss the next ancestral feast. Without looking at the man Okonkwo had said: 'This meeting is for men.' The man who had contradicted him had no titles. That was why he had called him a woman. Okonkwo knew how to kill a man's spirit.

Everybody at the kindred meeting took sides with Osugo when Okonkwo called him a woman. The oldest man present said sternly that those whose palm-kernels were cracked for them by a benevolent spirit should not forget to be humble. Okonkwo said he was sorry for what he had said, and the meeting continued.

But it was really not true that Okonkwo's palm-kernels had been cracked for him by a benevolent spirit. He had cracked them himself. Anyone who knew his grim struggle against poverty and misfortune could not say he had been lucky. If ever a man deserved his success, that man was Okonkwo. At an early age he had achieved fame as the greatest wrestler in all the land. That was not luck. At the most one could say that his *chi* or personal god was good. But the Ibo people have a proverb that when a man says yes his *chi* says yes also. Okonkwo said yes very strongly; so his *chi* agreed. And not only his *chi* but his clan too, because it judged a man by the work of his hands. That was why Okonkwo had been chosen by the nine villages to carry a message of war to their enemies unless they agreed to give up a

19

young man and a virgin to atone for the murder of Udo's wife. And such was the deep fear that their enemies had for Umuofia that they treated Okonkwo like a king and brought him a virgin who was given to Udo as wife, and the lad Ikemefuna.

◆

The elders of the clan had decided that Ikemefuna should be in Okonkwo's care for a while. But no one thought it would be as long as three years. They seemed to forget all about him as soon as they had taken the decision.

At first Ikemefuna was very much afraid. Once or twice he tried to run away, but he did not know where to begin. He thought of his mother and his three-year-old sister and wept bitterly. Nwoye's mother was very kind to him and treated him as one of her own children. But all he said was: 'When shall I go home?' When Okonkwo heard that he would not eat any food he came into the hut with a big stick in his hand and stood over him while he swallowed his yams, trembling. A few moments later he went behind the hut and began to vomit painfully. Nwoye's mother went to him and placed her hands on his chest and on his back. He was ill for three market weeks, and when he recovered he seemed to have overcome his great fear and sadness.

He was by nature a very lively boy and he gradually became popular in Okonkwo's household, especially with the children. Okonkwo's son, Nwoye, who was two years younger, became quite inseparable from him because he seemed to know everything. He could fashion out flutes from bamboo stems and even from the elephant grass. He knew the names of all the birds and could set clever traps for the little bush rodents. And he knew which trees made the strongest bows.

Even Okonkwo himself became very fond of the boy – inwardly of course. Okonkwo never showed any emotion openly, unless it be the emotion of anger. To show affection was a sign of weakness; the only thing worth demonstrating was strength. He therefore treated Ikemefuna as he treated everybody else – with a heavy hand. But there was no doubt that he liked the boy. Sometimes when he went to big village meetings or communal ancestral feasts he allowed Ikemefuna to accompany him, like a son, carrying his stool and his goatskin bag. And, indeed, Ikemefuna called him father.

◆

Ikemefuna came to Umuofia at the end of the carefree season between harvest and planting. In fact he recovered from his illness only a few days before the Week of Peace began. And that was also the year Okonkwo broke the peace, and was punished, as was the custom, by Ezeani, the priest of the earth goddess.

Okonkwo was provoked to justifiable anger by his youngest wife, who went to plait her hair at her friend's house and did not return early enough to cook the afternoon meal. Okonkwo did not know at first that she was not at home. After waiting in vain for the dish he went to her hut to see what she was doing. There was nobody in the hut and the fireplace was cold.

'Where is Ojiugo?' he asked his second wife, who came out of her hut to draw water from the gigantic pot in the shade of a small tree in the middle of the compound.

'She has gone to plait her hair.'

Okonkwo bit his lips as anger welled up within him.

'Where are her children? Did she take them?' he asked with unusual coolness and restraint.

'They are here,' answered his first wife, Nwoye's mother. Okonkwo bent down and looked into her hut. Ojiugo's children were eating with the children of his first wife.

'Did she ask you to feed them before she went?'

'Yes,' lied Nwoye's mother, trying to minimise Ojiugo's thoughtlessness.

Okonkwo knew she was not speaking the truth. He walked back to his *obi* to wait Ojiugo's return. And when she returned he beat her very heavily. In his anger he had forgotten that it was the Week of Peace. His first two wives ran out in great alarm pleading with him that it was the sacred week. But Okonkwo was not the man to stop beating somebody half-way through, not even for fear of a goddess.

Okonkwo's neighbours heard his wife crying and sent their voices over the compound walls to ask what was the matter. Some of them came over to see for themselves. It was unheard of to beat somebody during the sacred week.

Before it was dusk Ezeani, who was the priest of the earth goddess, Ani, called on Okonkwo in his *obi*. Okonkwo brought out kola nut and placed it before the priest.

'Take away your kola nut. I shall not eat in the house of a man who has no respect for our gods and ancestors.'

Okonkwo tried to explain to him what his wife had done, but Ezeani seemed to pay no attention. He held a short staff in his hand which he brought down on the floor to emphasize his points.

'Listen to me,' he said when Okonkwo had spoken. 'You are not a stranger in Umuofia. You know as well as I do that our forefathers ordained that before we plant any crops in the earth we should observe a week in which a man does not say a harsh word to his neighbour. We live in peace with our fellows to honour our great goddess of the earth without whose blessing our crops will not grow. You have committed a great evil.' He brought down his staff heavily on the floor. 'You wife was at fault, but even if you came into your *obi* and found her lover on top of her, you would still have committed a great evil to beat her.' His staff came down again. 'The evil you have done can ruin the whole clan. The earth goddess whom you have insulted may refuse to give us her increase, and we shall all perish.' His tone now changed from anger to command. 'You will bring to the shrine of Ani tomorrow one she-goat, one hen, a length of cloth and a hundred cowries.' He rose and left the hut.

Okonkwo did as the priest said. He also took with him a pot of palm-wine. Inwardly, he was repentant. But he was not the man to go about telling his neighbours that he was in error. And so people said he had no respect for the gods of the clan. His enemies said his good fortune had gone to his head. They called him the little bird *nza* who so far forgot himself after a heavy meal that he challenged his *chi*.

No work was done during the Week of Peace. People called on their neighbours and drank palm-wine. This year they talked of nothing else but the *nso-ani* which Okonkwo had committed. It was the first time for many years that a man had broken the sacred peace. Even the oldest men could only remember one or two other occasions somewhere in the dim past.

22

Ogbuefi Ezeudu, who was the oldest man in the village, was telling two other men who came to visit him that the punishment for breaking the Peace of Ani had become very mild in their clan.

'It has not always been so,' he said. 'My father told me that he had been told that in the past a man who broke the peace was dragged on the ground through the village until he died. But after a while this custom was stopped because it spoilt the peace which it was meant to preserve.'

'Somebody told me yesterday,' said one of the younger men, 'that in some clans it is an abomination for a man to die during the Week of Peace.'

'It is indeed true,' said Ogbuefi Ezeudu. 'They have that custom in Obodoani. If a man dies at this time he is not buried but cast into the Evil Forest. It is a bad custom which these people observe because they lack understanding. They throw away large numbers of men and women without burial. And what is the result? Their clan is full of the evil spirits of these unburied dead, hungry to do harm to the living.'

◆

After the Week of Peace every man and his family began to clear the bush to make new farms. The cut bush was left to dry and fire was then set to it. As the smoke rose into the sky kites appeared from different directions and hovered over the burning field in silent valediction. The rainy season was approaching when they would go away until the dry season returned.

Okonkwo spent the next few days preparing his seed-yams. He looked at each yam carefully to see whether it was good for sowing. Sometimes he decided that a yam was too big to be sown as one seed and he split it deftly along its length with his sharp knife. His eldest son, Nwoye, and Ikemefuna helped him by fetching the yams in long baskets from the barn and in counting the prepared seeds in groups of four hundred. Sometimes Okonkwo gave them a few yams each to prepare. But he always found fault with their effort, and he said so with much threatening.

'Do you think you are cutting up yams for cooking?' he asked Nwoye. 'If you split another yam of this size, I shall break your jaw.

23

You think you are still a child. I began to own a farm at your age. And you,' he said to Ikemefuna, 'do you not grow yams where you come from?'

Inwardly Okonkwo knew that the boys were still too young to understand fully the difficult art of preparing seed-yams. But he thought that one could not begin too early. Yam stood for manliness, and he who could feed his family on yams from one harvest to another was a very great man indeed. Okonkwo wanted his son to be a great farmer and a great man. He would stamp out the disquieting signs of laziness which he thought he already saw in him.

'I will not have a son who cannot hold up his head in the gathering of the clan. I would sooner strangle him with my own hands. And if you stand staring at me like that,' he swore, 'Amadiora will break your head for you!'

Some days later, when the land had been moistened by two or three heavy rains, Okonkwo and his family went to the farm with baskets of seed-yams, their hoes and matchets, and the planting began. They made single mounds of earth in straight lines all over the field and sowed the yams in them.

Yam, the king of crops, was a very exacting king. For three or four moons it demanded hard work and constant attention from cock-crow till the chickens went back to roost. The young tendrils were protected from earth-heat with rings of sisal leaves. As the rains became heavier the women planted maize, melons and beans between the yam mounds. The yams were then staked, first with little sticks and later with tall and big tree branches. The women weeded the farm three times at definite periods in the life of the yams, neither early nor late.

And now the rains had really come, so heavy and persistent that even the village rain-maker no longer claimed to be able to intervene. He could not stop the rain now, just as he would not attempt to start it in the heart of the dry season, without serious danger to his own health. The personal dynamism required to counter the forces of these extremes of weather would be far too great for the human frame.

And so nature was not interfered with in the middle of the rainy season. Sometimes it poured down in such thick sheets of water that earth and sky seemed merged in one grey wetness. It was then

24

uncertain whether the low rumbling of Amadiora's thunder came from above or below. At such times, in each of the countless thatched huts of Umuofia, children sat around their mother's cooking fire telling stories, or with their father in his *obi* warming themselves from a log fire, roasting and eating maize. It was a brief resting period between the exacting and arduous planting season and the equally exacting but light-hearted month of harvests.

◆

Ikemefuna had begun to feel like a member of Okonkwo's family. He still thought about his mother and his three-year-old sister, and he had moments of sadness and depression. But he and Nwoye had become so deeply attached to each other that such moments became less frequent and less poignant. Ikemefuna had an endless stock of folk tales. Even those which Nwoye knew already were told with a new freshness and the local flavour of a different clan. Nwoye remembered this period very vividly till the end of his life. He even remembered how he had laughed when Ikemefuna told him that the proper name for a corn-cob with only a few scattered grains was *eze-agadi-nwayi*, or the teeth of an old woman. Nwoye's mind had gone immediately to Nwayieke, who lived near the udala tree. She had about three teeth and was always smoking her pipe.

Gradually the rains became lighter and less frequent, and earth and sky once again became separate. The rain fell in thin, slanting showers through sunshine and quiet breeze. Children no longer stayed indoors but ran about singing:

> 'The rain is falling, the sun is shining,
> Alone Nnadi is cooking and eating.'

Nwoye always wondered who Nnadi was and why he should live all by himself, cooking and eating. In the end he decided that Nnadi must live in that land of Ikemefuna's favourite story where the ant holds his court in splendour and the sands dance for ever.

Chapter Five

The Feast of the New Yam was approaching and Umuofia was in a festival mood. It was an occasion for giving thanks to Ani, the earth goddess and the source of all fertility. Ani played a greater part in the life of the people than any other deity. She was the ultimate judge of morality and conduct. And what was more, she was in close communion with the departed fathers of the clan whose bodies had been committed to earth.

The Feast of the New Yam was held every year before the harvest began, to honour the earth goddess and the ancestral spirits of the clan. New yams could not be eaten until some had first been offered to these powers. Men and women, young and old, looked forward to the New Yam Festival because it began the season of plenty – the new year. On the last night before the festival, yams of the old year were all disposed of by those who still had them. The new year must begin with tasty, fresh yams and not the shrivelled and fibrous crop of the previous year. All cooking-pots, calabashes and wooden bowls were thoroughly washed, especially the wooden mortar in which yam was pounded. Yam foo-foo and vegetable soup was the chief food in the celebration. So much of it was cooked that, no matter how heavily the family ate or how many friends and relations they invited from neighbouring villages, there was always a huge quantity of food left over at the end of the day. The story was always told of a wealthy man who set before his guests a mount of foo-foo so high that those who sat on one side could not see what was happening on the other, and it was not until late in the evening that one of them saw for the first time his in-law who had arrived during the course of the meal and had fallen to on the opposite side. It was only then that they exchanged greetings and shook hands over what was left of the food.

The New Yam Festival was thus an occasion for joy throughout

Umuofia. And every man whose arm was strong, as the Ibo people say, was expected to invite large numbers of guests from far and wide. Okonkwo always asked his wives' relations, and since he now had three wives his guests would make a fairly big crowd.

But somehow Okonkwo could never become as enthusiastic over feasts as most people. He was a good eater and he could drink one or two fairly big gourds of palm-wine. But he was always uncomfortable sitting around for days waiting for a feast or getting over it. He would be very much happier working on his farm.

The festival was now only three days away. Okonkwo's wives had scrubbed the walls and the huts with red earth until they reflected light. They had then drawn patterns on them in white, yellow and dark green. They then set about painting themselves with cam wood and drawing beautiful black patterns on their stomachs and on their backs. The children were also decorated, especially their hair, which was shaved in beautiful patterns. The three women talked excitedly about the relations who had been invited, and the children revelled in the thought of being spoilt by these visitors from mother-land. Ikemefuna was equally excited. The New Yam Festival seemed to him to be a much bigger event here than in his own village, a place which was already becoming remote and vague in his imagination.

And then the storm burst. Okonkwo, who had been walking about aimlessly in his compound in suppressed anger, suddenly found an outlet.

'Who killed this banana tree?' he asked.

A hush fell on the compound immediately.

'Who killed this tree? Or are you all deaf and dumb?'

As a matter of fact the three was very much alive. Okonkwo's second wife had merely cut a few leaves off it to wrap some food, and she said so. Without further argument Okonkwo gave her a sound beating and left her and her only daughter weeping. Neither of the other wives dared to interfere beyond an occasional and tentative, 'It is enough, Okonkwo,' pleaded from a reasonable distance.

His anger thus satisfied, Okonkwo decided to go out hunting. He had an old rusty gun made by a clever blacksmith who had come to live in Umuofia long ago. But although Okonkwo was a great man whose prowess was universally acknowledged, he was not a hunter.

In fact he had not killed a rat with his gun. And so when he called Ikemefuna to fetch his gun, the wife who had just been beaten murmured something about guns that never shot. Unfortunately for her, Okonkwo heard it and ran madly into his room for the loaded gun, ran out again and aimed at her as she clambered over the dwarf wall of the barn. He pressed the trigger and there was a loud report accompanied by the wail of his wives and children. He threw down the gun and jumped into the barn, and there lay the woman, very much shaken and frightened but quite unhurt. He heaved a heavy sigh and went away with the gun.

In spite of this incident the New Yam Festival was celebrated with great joy in Okonkwo's household. Early that morning as he offered a sacrifice of new yam and palm-oil to his ancestors he asked them to protect him, his children and their mothers in the new year.

As the day wore on his in-laws arrived from three surrounding villages, and each party brought with them a huge pot of palm-wine. And there was eating and drinking till night, when Okonkwo's in-laws began to leave for their homes.

◆

The second day of the new year was the day of the great wrestling match between Okonkwo's village and their neighbours. It was difficult to say which the people enjoyed more – the feasting and fellowship of the first day or the wrestling contest of the second. But there was one woman who had no doubt whatever in her mind. She was Okonkwo's second wife, Ekwefi, whom he nearly shot. There was no festival in all the seasons of the year which gave her as much pleasure as the wrestling match. Many years ago when she was the village beauty Okonkwo had won her heart by throwing the Cat in the greatest contest within living memory. She did not marry him because he was too poor to pay her bride-price. But a few years later she ran away from her husband and came to live with Okonkwo. All this happened many years ago. Now Ekwefi was a woman of forty-five who had suffered a great deal in her time. But her love of wrestling contests was still as strong as it was thirty years ago.

It was not yet noon on the second day of the New Yam Festival.

Ekwefi and her only daughter, Ezinma, sat near the fireplace waiting for the water in the pot to boil. The fowl Ekwefi had just killed was in the wooden mortar. The water began to boil, and in one deft movement she lifted the pot from the fire and poured the boiling water on to the fowl. She put back the empty pot on the circular pad in the corner, and looked at her palms, which were black with soot. Ezinma was always surprised that her mother could lift a pot from the fire with her bare hands.

'Ekwefi,' she said, 'is it true that when people are grown up, fire does not burn them?' Ezinma, unlike most children, called her mother by her name.

'Yes,' replied Ekwefi, too busy to argue. Her daughter was only ten years old but she was wiser than her years.

'But Nwoye's mother dropped her pot of hot soup the other day and it broke on the floor.'

Ekwefi turned the hen over in the mortar and began to pluck the feathers.

'Ekwefi,' said Ezinma, who had joined in plucking the feathers, 'my eyelid is twitching.'

'It means you are going to cry,' said her mother.

'No,' Ezinma said, 'it is this eyelid, the top one.'

'That means you will see something.'

'What will I see?' she asked.

'How can I know?' Ekwefi wanted her to work it out herself.

'Oho,' said Ezinma at last. 'I know what it is – the wrestling match.'

At last the hen was plucked clean. Ekwefi tried to pull out the horny beak but it was too hard. She turned round on her low stool and put the beak in the fire for a few moments. She pulled again and it came off.

'Ekwefi!' a voice called from one of the other huts. It was Nwoye's mother, Okonkwo's first wife.

'Is that me?' Ekwefi called back. That was the way people answered calls from outside. They never answered yes for fear it might be an evil spirit calling.

'Will you give Ezinma some fire to bring to me?' Her own children and Ikemefuna had gone to the stream.

Ekwefi put a few live coals into a piece of broken pot and Ezinma carried it across the clean-swept compound to Nwoye's mother.

'Thank you, Nma,' she said. She was peeling new yams, and in a basket beside her were green vegetables and beans.

'Let me make the fire for you,' Ezinma offered.

'Thank you, Ezigbo,' she said. She often called her Ezigbo, which means 'the good one'.

Ezinma went outside and brought some sticks from a huge bundle of firewood. She broke them into little pieces across the sole of her foot and began to build a fire, blowing it with her breath.

'You will blow your eyes out,' said Nwoye's mother, looking up from the yams she was peeling. 'Use the fan.' She stood up and pulled out the fan which was fastened into one of the rafters. As soon as she got up, the troublesome nanny-goat, which had been dutifully eating yam peelings, dug her teeth into the real thing, scooped out two mouthfuls and fled from the hut to chew the cud in the goats' shed. Nwoye's mother swore at her and settled down again to her peeling. Ezinma's fire was now sending up thick clouds of smoke. She went on fanning it until it burst into flames. Nwoye's mother thanked her and she went back to her mother's hut.

Just then the distant beating of drums began to reach them. It came from the direction of the *ilo*, the village playground. Every village had its own *ilo* which was as old as the village itself and where all the great ceremonies and dances took place. The drums beat the unmistakable wrestling dance – quick, light and gay, and it came floating on the wind.

Okonkwo cleared his throat and moved his feet to the beat of the drums. It filled him with fire as it had always done from his youth. He trembled with the desire to conquer and subdue. It was like the desire for woman.

'We shall be late for the wrestling,' said Ezinma to her mother.

'They will not begin until the sun goes down.'

'But they are beating the drums.'

'Yes. The drums begin at noon but the wrestling waits until the sun begins to sink. Go and see if your father has brought out yams for the afternoon.'

'He has. Nwoye's mother is already cooking.'

'Go and bring our own, then. We must cook quickly or we shall be late for the wrestling.'

Ezinma ran in the direction of the barn and brought back two yams from the dwarf wall.

Ekwefi peeled the yams quickly. The troublesome nanny-goat sniffed about, eating the peelings. She cut the yams into small pieces and began to prepare a pottage, using some of the chicken.

At that moment they heard someone crying just outside their compound. It was very much like Obiageli, Nwoye's sister.

'Is that not Obiageli weeping?' Ekwefi called across the yard to Nwoye's mother.

'Yes,' she replied. 'She must have broken her water-pot.'

The weeping was now quite close and soon the children filed in, carrying on their heads various sizes of pots suitable to their years. Ikemefuna came first with the biggest pot, closely followed by Nwoye and his two younger brothers. Obiageli brought up the rear, her face streaming with tears. In her hand was the cloth pad on which the pot should have rested on her head.

'What happened?' her mother asked, and Obiageli told her mournful story. Her mother consoled her and promised to buy her another pot.

Nwoye's younger brothers were about to tell their mother the true story of the accident when Ikemefuna looked at them sternly and they held their peace. The fact was that Obiageli had been making *inyanga* with her pot. She had balanced it on her head, folded her arms in front of her and began to sway her waist like a grown-up young lady. When the pot fell down and broke she burst out laughing. She only began to weep when they got near the iroko tree outside their compound.

The drums were still beating, persistent and unchanging. Their sound was no longer a separate thing from the living village. It was like the pulsation of its heart. It throbbed in the air, in the sunshine, and even in the trees, and filled the village with excitement.

Ekwefi ladled her husband's share of the pottage into a bowl and covered it. Ezinma took it to him in his *obi*.

Okonkwo was sitting on a goatskin already eating his first wife's meal. Obiageli, who had brought it from her mother's hut, sat on the

31

floor waiting for him to finish. Ezinma placed her mother's dish before him and sat with Obiageli.

'Sit like a woman!' Okonkwo shouted at her. Ezinma brought her two legs together and stretched them in front of her.

'Father, will you go to see the wrestling?' Ezinma asked after a suitable interval.

Yes,' he answered. 'Will you go?'

'Yes.' And after a pause she said: 'Can I bring your chair for you?'

'No, that is a boy's job.' Okonkwo was specially fond of Ezinma. She looked very much like her mother, who was once the village beauty. But his fondness only showed on very rare occasions.

'Obiageli broke her pot today,' Ezinma said.

'Yes, she has told me about it,' Okonkwo said between mouthfuls.

'Father,' said Obiageli, 'people should not talk when they are eating or pepper may go down the wrong way.'

'That is very true. Do you hear that, Ezinma? You are older than Obiageli but she has more sense.'

He uncovered his second wife's dish and began to eat from it. Obiageli took the first dish and returned to her mother's hut. And then Nkechi came in, bringing the third dish. Nkechi was the daughter of Okonkwo's third wife.

In the distance the drums continued to beat.

Chapter Six

The whole village turned out on the *ilo*, men, women and children. They stood round in a huge circle leaving the centre of the playground free. The elders and grandees of the village sat on their own stools brought there by their young sons or slaves. Okonkwo was among them. All others stood except those who came early enough to secure places on the few stands which had been built by placing smooth logs on forked pillars.

The wrestlers were not there yet and the drummers held the field. They too sat just in front of the huge circle of spectators, facing the elders. Behind them was the big and ancient silk-cotton tree which was sacred. Spirits of good children lived in that tree waiting to be born. On ordinary days young women who desired children came to sit under its shade.

There were seven drums and they were arranged according to their sizes in a long wooden basket. Three men beat them with sticks, working feverishly from one drum to another. They were possessed by the spirit of the drums.

The young men who kept order on these occasions dashed about, consulting among themselves and with the leaders of the two wrestling teams, who were still outside the circle, behind the crowd. Once in a while two young men carrying palm fronds ran round the circle and kept the crowd back by beating the ground in front of them or, if they were stubborn, their legs and feets.

At last the two teams danced into the circle and the crowd roared and clapped. The drums rose to a frenzy. The people surged forwards. The young men who kept order flew around, waving their palm fronds. Old men nodded to the beat of the drums and remembered the days when they wrestled to its intoxicating rhythm.

The contest began with boys of fifteen or sixteen. There were only

33

three such boys in each team. They were not the real wrestlers; they merely set the scene. Within a short time the first two bouts were over. But the third created a big sensation even among the elders who did not usually show their excitement so openly. It was as quick as the other two, perhaps even quicker. But very few people had ever seen that kind of wrestling before. As soon as the two boys closed in, one of them did something which no one could describe because it had been as quick as a flash. And the other boy was flat on his back. The crowd roared and clapped and for a while drowned the frenzied drums. Okonkwo sprang to his feet and quickly sat down again. Three young men from the victorious boy's team ran forward, carried him shoulder-high and danced through the cheering crowd. Everybody soon knew who the boy was. His name was Maduka, the son of Obierika.

The drummers stopped for a brief rest before the real matches. Their bodies shone with sweat, and they took up fans and began to fan themselves. They also drank water from small pots and ate kola nuts. They became ordinary human beings again, talking and laughing among themselves and with others who stood near them. The air, which had been stretched taut with excitement, relaxed again. It was as if water had been poured on the tightened skin of a drum. Many people looked around, perhaps for the first time, and saw those who stood or sat next to them.

'I did not know it was you,' Ekwefi said to the woman who had stood shoulder to shoulder with her since the beginning of the matches.

'I do not blame you,' said the woman. 'I have never seen such a large crowd of people. Is it true that Okonkwo nearly killed you with his gun?'

'It is true indeed, my dear friend. I cannot yet find a mouth with which to tell the story.'

'Your *chi* is very much awake, my friend. And how is my daughter, Ezinma?'

'She has been very well for some time now. Perhaps she has come to stay.'

'I think she has. How old is she now?'

'She is about ten years old.'

34

'I think she will stay. They usually stay if they do not die before the age of six.'

'I pray she stays,' said Ekwefi with a heavy sigh.

The woman with whom she talked was called Chielo. She was the priestess of Agbala, the Oracle of the Hills and the Caves. In ordinary life Chielo was a widow with two children. She was very friendly with Ekwefi and they shared a common shed in the market. She was particularly fond of Ekwefi's only daughter, Ezinma, whom she called 'my daughter'. Quite often she bought bean-cakes and gave Ekwefi some to take home to Ezinma. Anyone seeing Chielo in ordinary life would hardly believe she was the same person who prophesied when the spirit of Agbala was upon her.

◆

The drummers took up their sticks again and the air shivered and grew tense like a tightened bow.

The two teams were ranged facing each other across the clear space. A young man from one team danced across the centre to the other side and pointed at whomever he wanted to fight. They danced back to the centre together and then closed in.

There were twelve men on each side and the challenge went from one side to the other. Two judges walked around the wrestlers and when they thought they were equally matched, stopped them. Five matches ended in this way. But the really exciting moments were when a man was thrown. The huge voice of the crowd then rose to the sky and in every direction. It was even heard in the surrounding villages.

The last match was between the leaders of the teams. They were among the best wrestlers in all the nine villages. The crowd wondered who would throw the other this year. Some said Okafo was the better man; others said he was not the equal of Ikezue. Last year neither of them had thrown the other even though the judges had allowed the contest to go on longer than was the custom. They had the same style and one saw the other's plans beforehand. It might happen again this year.

Dusk was already approaching when their contest began. The drums went mad and the crowds also. They surged forward as the two young men danced into the circle. The palm fronds were helpless in keeping them back.

Ikezue held out his right hand. Okafo seized it, and they closed in. It was a fierce contest. Ikezue strove to dig in his right heel behind Okafo so as to pitch him backwards in the clever *ege* style. But the one knew what the other was thinking. The crowd had surrounded and swallowed up the drummers, whose frantic rhythm was no longer a mere disembodied sound but the very heart-beat of the people.

The wrestlers were now almost still in each other's grip. The muscles on their arms and their thighs and on their backs stood out and twitched. It looked like an equal match. The two judges were already moving forward to separate them when Ikezue, now desperate, went down quickly on one knee in an attempt to fling his man backwards over his head. It was a sad miscalculation. Quick as the lightning of Amadiora, Okafo raised his right leg and swung it over his rival's head. The crowd burst into a thunderous roar. Okafo was swept off his feet by his supporters and carried home shoulder-high. They sang his praise and the young women clapped their hands:

> *'Who will wrestle for our village?*
> *Okafo will wrestle for our village.*
> *Has he thrown a hundred men?*
> *He has thrown four hundred men.*
> *Has he thrown a hundred Cats?*
> *He has thrown four hundred Cats.*
> *Then send him word to fight for us.'*

Chapter Seven

For three years Ikemefuna lived in Okonkwo's household and the elders of Umuofia seemed to have forgotten about him. He grew rapidly like a yam tendril in the rainy season, and was full of the sap of life. He had become wholly absorbed into his new family. He was like an elder brother to Nwoye, and from the very first seemed to have kindled a new fire in the younger boy. He made him feel grown-up; and they no longer spent the evenings in mother's hut while she cooked, but now sat with Okonkwo in his *obi*, or watched him as he tapped his palm tree for the evening wine. Nothing pleased Nwoye now more than to be sent for by his mother or another of his father's wives to do one of those difficult and masculine tasks in the home, like splitting wood, or pounding food. On receiving such a message through a younger brother or sister, Nwoye would feign annoyance and grumble aloud about women and their troubles.

Okonkwo was inwardly pleased at his son's development, and he knew it was due to Ikemefuna. He wanted Nwoye to grow into a tough young man capable of ruling his father's household when he was dead and gone to join the ancestors. He wanted him to be a prosperous man, having enough in his barn to feed the ancestors with regular sacrifices. And so he was always happy when he heard him grumbling about women. That showed that in time he would be able to control his women-folk. No matter how prosperous a man was, if he was unable to rule his women and his children (and especially his women) he was not really a man. He was like the man in the song who had ten and one wives and not enough soup for his foo-foo.

So Okonkwo encouraged the boys to sit with him in his *obi*, and he told them stories of the land – masculine stories of violence and bloodshed. Nwoye knew that it was right to be masculine and to be violent, but somehow he still preferred the stories that his mother used to tell, and which she no doubt still told to her younger children – stories of the tortoise and his wily ways, and of the bird *eneke-nti-oba* who challenged the whole world to a wrestling contest and was finally thrown by the cat. He remembered the story she often told of the quarrel between Earth and Sky long ago, and how Sky withheld rain for seven years, until crops withered and the dead could not be buried because the hoes broke on the stony Earth. At last Vulture was sent to plead with Sky, and to soften his heart with a song of the suffering of the sons of men. Whenever Nwoye's mother sang this song he felt carried away to the distant scene in the sky where Vulture, Earth's emissary, sang for mercy. At last Sky was moved to pity, and he gave to Vulture rain wrapped in leaves of coco-yam. But as he flew home his long talon pierced the leaves and the rain fell as it had never fallen before. And so heavily did it rain on Vulture that he did not return to deliver his message but flew to a distant land, from where he had espied a fire. And when he got there he found it was a man making a sacrifice. He warmed himself in the fire and ate the entrails.

That was the kind of story that Nwoye loved. But he now knew that they were for foolish women and children, and he knew that his father wanted him to be a man. And so he feigned that he no longer cared for women's stories. And when he did this he saw that his father was pleased, and no longer rebuked him or beat him. So Nwoye and Ikemefuna would listen to Okonkwo's stories about tribal wars or how, years ago, he had stalked his victim, overpowered him and obtained his first human head. And as he told them of the past they sat in darkness or the dim glow of logs, waiting for the women to finish their cooking. When they finished, each brought her bowl of foo-foo and bowl of soup to her husband. An oil lamp was lit and Okonkwo tasted from each bowl, and then passed two shares to Nwoye and Ikemefuna.

In this way the moons and the seasons passed. And then the locusts came. It had not happened for many a long year. The elders said locusts came once in a generation, reappeared every year for seven years and then disappeared for another lifetime. They went back to their caves in a distant land, where they were guarded by a race of stunted men. And then after another lifetime these men opened the caves again and the locusts came to Umuofia.

They came in the cold harmattan season after the harvests had been gathered, and ate up all the wild grass in the fields.

Okonkwo and the two boys were working on the red outer walls of the compound. This was one of the lighter tasks of the after-harvest season. A new cover of thick palm branches and palm leaves was set on the walls to protect them from the next rainy season. Okonkwo worked on the outside of the wall and the boys worked from within. There were little holes from one side to the other in the upper levels of the wall, and through these Okonkwo passed the rope, or *tie-tie*, to the boys and they passed it round the wooden stays and then back to him; and in this way the cover was strengthened on the wall.

The women had gone to the bush to collect firewood, and the little children to visit their playmates in the neighbouring compounds. The harmattan was in the air and seemed to distil a hazy feeling of sleep on the world. Okonkwo and the boys worked in complete silence, which was only broken when a new palm frond was lifted on to the wall or when a busy hen moved dry leaves about in her ceaseless search for food.

And then quite suddenly a shadow fell on the world, and the sun seemed hidden behind a thick cloud. Okonkwo looked up from his work and wondered if it was going to rain at such an unlikely time of the year. But almost immediately a shout of joy broke out in all directions, and Umuofia, which had dozed in the noon-day haze, broke into life and activity.

'Locusts are descending,' was joyfully chanted everywhere, and men, women and children left their work or their play and ran into the open to see the unfamiliar sight. The locusts had not come for many, many years, and only the old people had seen them before.

At first, a fairly small swarm came. They were the harbingers sent to survey the land. And then appeared on the horizon a slowly-moving mass like a boundless sheet of black cloud drifting towards Umuofia. Soon it covered half the sky, and the solid mass was now broken by tiny eyes of light like shining star-dust. It was a tremendous sight, full of power and beauty.

Everyone was now about, talking excitedly and praying that the locusts should camp in Umuofia for the night. For although locusts had not visited Umuofia for many years, everybody knew by instinct that they were very good to eat. And at last the locusts did descend. They settled on every tree and on every blade of grass; they settled on the roofs and covered the bare ground. Mighty tree branches broke away under them, and the whole country became the brown-earth colour of the vast, hungry swarm.

Many people went out with baskets trying to catch them, but the elders counselled patience till nightfall. And they were right. The locusts settled in the bushes for the night and their wings became wet with dew. Then all Umuofia turned out in spite of the cold harmattan, and everyone filled his bags and pots with locusts. The next morning they were roasted in clay pots and then spread in the sun until they became dry and brittle. And for many days this rare food was eaten with solid palm-oil.

Okonkwo sat in his *obi* crunching happily with Ikemefuna and Nwoye, and drinking palm-wine copiously, when Ogbuefi Ezeudu came in. Ezeudu was the oldest man in this quarter of Umuofia. He had been a great and fearless warrior in his time, and was now accorded great respect in all the clan. He refused to join in the meal, and asked Okonkwo to have a word with him outside. And so they walked out together, the old man supporting himself with his stick. When they were out of ear-shot, he said to Okonkwo:

'That boy calls you father. Do not bear a hand in his death.' Okonkwo was surprised, and was about to say something when the old man continued:

'Yes, Umuofia has decided to kill him. The Oracle of the Hills and the Caves has pronounced it. They will take him outside Umuofia as is the custom, and kill him there. But I want you to have nothing to do with it. He calls you his father.'

The next day a group of elders from all the nine villages of Umuofia came to Okonkwo's house early in the morning, and before they began to speak in low tones Nwoye and Ikemefuna were sent out. They did not stay very long, but when they went away Okonkwo sat still for a very long time supporting his chin in his palms. Later in the day he called Ikemefuna and told him that he was to be taken home the next day. Nwoye overheard it and burst into tears, whereupon his father beat him heavily. As for Ikemefuna, he was at a loss. His own home had gradually become very faint and distant. He still missed his mother and his sister and would be very glad to see them. But

40

somehow he knew he was not going to see them. He remembered once when men had talked in low tones with his father; and it seemed now as if it was happening all over again.

Later, Nwoye went to his mother's hut and told her that Ikemufuna was going home. She immediately dropped the pestle with which she was grinding pepper, folded her arms across her breast and sighed, 'Poor child.'

The next day, the men returned with a pot of wine. They were all fully dressed as if they were going to a big clan meeting or to pay a visit to a neighbouring village. They passed their cloths under the right arm-pit, and hung their goatskin bags and sheathed matchets over their left shoulders. Okonkwo got ready quickly and the party set out with Ikemefuna carrying the pot of wine. A deathly silence descended on Okonkwo's compound. Even the very little children seemed to know. Throughout that day Nwoye sat in his mother's hut and tears stood in his eyes.

At the beginning of their journey the men of Umuofia talked and laughed about the locusts, about their women, and about some effeminate men who had refused to come with them. But as they drew near to the outskirts of Umuofia silence fell upon them too.

The sun rose slowly to the centre of the sky, and the dry, sandy footway began to throw up the heat that lay buried in it. Some birds chirruped in the forests around. The men trod dry leaves on the sand. All else was silent. Then from the distance came the faint beating of the *ekwe*. It rose and faded with the wind – a peaceful dance from a distant clan.

'It is an *ozo* dance,' the men said among themselves. But no one was sure where it was coming from. Some said Ezimili, others Abame or Aninta. They argued for a short while and fell into silence again, and the elusive dance rose and fell with the wind. Somewhere a man was taking one of the titles of his clan, with music and dancing and a great feast.

The footway had now become a narrow line in the heart of the forest. The short trees and sparse undergrowth which surrounded the men's village began to give way to giant trees and climbers which perhaps had stood from the beginning of things, untouched by the axe and the bush-fire. The sun breaking through their leaves and branches threw a pattern of light and shade on the sandy footway.

Ikemefuna heard a whisper close behind him and turned round sharply. The man who had whispered now called out aloud, urging the others to hurry up.

'We still have a long way to go,' he said. Then he and another man went before Ikemefuna and set a faster pace.

Thus the men of Umuofia pursued their way, armed with sheathed matchets, and Ikemefuna, carrying a pot of palm-wine on his head, walked in their midst. Although he had felt uneasy at first, he was not afraid now. Okonkwo walked behind him. He could hardly imagine that Okonkwo was not his real father. He had never been fond of his real father, and at the end of three years he had become very distant indeed. But his mother and his three-year-old sister . . . of course she would not be three now, but six. Would he recognize her now? She must have grown quite big. How his mother would weep for joy, and thank Okonkwo for having looked after him so well and for bringing him back. She would want to hear everything that had happened to him in all these years. Could he remember them all? He would tell her about Nwoye and his mother, and about the locusts . . . Then quite suddenly a thought came upon him. His mother might be dead. He tried in vain to force the thought out of his mind. Then he tried to settle the matter the way he used to settle such matters when he was a little boy. He still remembered the song:

> *Eze elina, elina!*
> *Sala*
> *Eze ilikwa ya*
> *Ikwaba akwa oligholi*
> *Ebe Danda nechi eze*
> *Ebe Uzuzu nete egwu*
> *Sala*

He sang it in his mind, and walked to its beat. If the song ended on his right foot, his mother was alive. If it ended on his left, she was dead. No, not dead, but ill. It ended on the right. She was alive and well. He sang the song again, and it ended on the left. But the second time did not count. The first voice gets to Chukwu, or God's house. That was a favourite saying of children. Ikemefuna felt like a child once more. It must be the thought of going home to his mother.

One of the men behind him cleared his throat. Ikemefuna looked back, and the man growled at him to go on and not stand looking back. The wav he said it sent cold fear down Ikemefuna's back. His hands trembled vaguely on the black pot he carried. Why had Okonkwo withdrawn to the rear? Ikemefuna felt his legs melting under him. And he was afraid to look back.

As the man who had cleared his throat drew up and raised his matchet, Okonkwo looked away. He heard the blow. The pot fell and broke in the sand. He heard Ikemefuna cry, 'My father, they have killed me!' as he ran towards him. Dazed with fear, Okonkwo drew his matchet and cut him down. He was afraid of being thought weak.

◆

As soon as his father walked in, that night, Nwoye knew that Ikemefuna had been killed, and something seemed to give way inside him, like the snapping of a tightened bow. He did not cry. He just hung limp. He had had the same kind of feeling not long ago, during the last harvest season. Every child loved the harvest season. Those who were big enough to carry even a few yams in a tiny basket went with grown-ups to the farm. And if they could not help in digging up the yams, they could gather firewood together for roasting the ones that would be eaten there on the farm. This roasted yam soaked in red palm-oil and eaten in the open farm was sweeter than any meal at home. It was after such a day at the farm during the last harvest that Nwoye had felt for the first time a snapping inside him like the one he now felt. They were returning home with baskets of yams from a distant farm across the stream when they had heard the voice of an infant crying in the thick forest. A sudden hush had fallen on the women, who had been talking, and they had quickened their steps. Nwoye had heard that twins were put in earthenware pots and thrown away in the forest, but he had never yet come across them. A vague chill had descended on him and his head had seemed to swell, like a solitary walker at night who passes an evil spirit on the way. Then something had given way inside him. It descended on him again, this feeling, when his father walked in, that night after killing Ikemefuna.

Chapter Eight

Okonkwo did not taste any food for two days after the death of Ikemefuna. He drank palm-wine from morning till night, and his eyes were red and fierce like the eyes of a rat when it was caught by the tail and dashed against the floor. He called his son, Nwoye, to sit with him in his *obi*. But the boy was afraid of him and slipped out of the hut as soon as he noticed him dozing.

He did not sleep at night. He tried not to think about Ikemefuna, but the more he tried the more he thought about him. Once he got up from bed and walked about his compound. But he was so weak that his legs could hardly carry him. He felt like a drunken giant walking with the limbs of a mosquito. Now and then a cold shiver descended on his head and spread down his body.

On the third day he asked his second wife, Ekwefi, to roast some plantains for him. She prepared then the way he liked – with slices of oil-bean and fish.

'You have not eaten for two days,' said his daughter Ezinma when she brought the food to him. 'So you must finish this.' She sat down and stretched her legs in front of her. Okonkwo ate the food absent-mindedly. 'She should have been a boy,' he thought as he looked at his ten-year-old daughter. He passed her a piece of fish.

'Go and bring me some cold water,' he said. Ezinma rushed out of the hut, chewing the fish, and soon returned with a bowl of cool water from the earthen pot in her mother's hut.

Okonkwo took the bowl from her and gulped the water down. He ate a few more pieces of plantain and pushed the dish aside.

'Bring me my bag,' he asked, and Ezinma brought his goatskin bag from the far end of the hut. He searched in it for his snuff-bottle. It was a deep bag and took almost the whole length of his arm. It contained other things apart from his snuff-bottle. There was a drinking horn in it, and also a drinking gourd, and they knocked against each other as he searched. When he brought out the snuff-bottle he tapped it a few times against his knee-cap before taking out some snuff on the palm of his left hand. Then he remembered that he had not taken out his snuff-spoon. He searched his bag again and brought out a small, flat, ivory spoon, with which he carried the brown snuff to his nostrils.

Ezinma took the dish in one hand and the empty water bowl in the other and went back to her mother's hut. 'She should have been a boy,' Okonkwo said to himself again. His mind went back to Ikemefuna and he shivered. If only he could find some work to do he would be able to forget. But it was the season of rest between the harvest and the next planting season. The only work that men did at this time was covering the walls of their compound with new palm fronds. And Okonkwo had already done that. He had finished it on the very day the locusts came, when he had worked on one side of the wall and Ikemefuna and Nwoye on the other.

'When did you become a shivering old woman,' Okonkwo asked himself, 'you are known in all the nine villages for your valour in war. How can a man who has killed five men in battle fall to pieces because he has added a boy to their number? Okonkwo, you have become a woman indeed.'

He sprang to his feet, hung his goatskin bag on his shoulder and went to visit his friend, Obierika.

Obierika was sitting outside under the shade of an orange tree making thatches from leaves of the raffia-palm. He exchanged greetings with Okonkwo and led the way into his *obi*.

'I was coming over to see you as soon as I finished that thatch,' he said, rubbing off the grains of sand that clung to his thighs.

'Is it well?' Okonkwo asked.

'Yes,' replied Obierika. 'My daughter's suitor is coming today and I hope we will clinch the matter of the bride-price. I want you to be there.'

Just then Obierika's son, Maduka, came into the *obi* from outside, greeted Okonkwo and turned towards the compound.

'Come and shake hands with me,' Okonkwo said to the lad. 'Your wrestling the other day gave me much happiness.' The boy smiled, shook hands with Okonkwo and went into the compound.

'He will do great things,' Okonkwo said. 'If I had a son like him I should be happy. I am worried about Nwoye. A bowl of pounded yams can throw him in a wrestling match. His two younger brothers are more promising. But I can tell you, Obierika, that my children do not resemble me. Where are the young suckers that will grow when the old banana tree dies? If Ezinma had been a boy I would have been happier. She has the right spirit.'

'You worry yourself for nothing,' said Obierika. 'The children are still very young.'

'Nwoye is old enough to impregnate a woman. At his age I was already fending for myself. No, my friend, he is not too young. A chick that will grow into a cock can be spotted the very day it hatches. I have done my best to make Nwoye grow into a man, but there is too much of his mother in him.'

'Too much of his grandfather,' Obierika thought, but he did not say it. The same thought also came to Okonkwo's mind. But he had long learnt how to lay that ghost. Whenever the thought of his father's weakness and failure troubled him he expelled it by thinking about his own strength and success. And so he did now. His mind went to his latest show of manliness.

'I cannot understand why you refused to come with us to kill that boy,' he asked Obierika.

'Because I did not want to,' Obierika replied sharply. 'I had something better to do.'

'You sound as if you question the authority and the decision of the Oracle, who said he should die.'

'I do not. Why should I? But the Oracle did not ask me to carry out its decision.'

'But someone had to do it. If we were all afraid of blood, it would not be done. And what do you think the Oracle would do then?'

'You know very well, Okonkwo, that I am not afraid of blood; and if anyone tells you that I am, he is telling a lie. And let me tell you one thing, my friend. If I were you I would have stayed at home. What you have done will not please the Earth. It is the kind of action for which the goddess wipes out whole families.'

'The Earth cannot punish me for obeying her messenger,' Okonkwo said. 'A child's fingers are not scalded by a piece of hot yam which its mother puts into its palm.'

'That is true,' Obierika agreed. 'But if the Oracle said that my son should be killed I would neither dispute it nor be the one to do it.'

They would have gone on arguing had Ofoedu not come in just then. It was clear from his twinkling eyes that he had important news. But it would be impolite to rush him. Obierika offered him a lobe of the kola nut he had broken with Okonkwo. Ofoedu ate slowly and talked about the locusts. When he finished his kola nut he said:

'The things that happen these days are very strange.'

'What has happened?' asked Okonkwo.

'Do you know Ogbuefi Ndulue?' Ofoedu asked.

'Ogbuefi Ndulue of Ire village,' Okonkwo and Obierika said together.

'He died this morning,' said Ofoedu.

'That is not strange. He was the oldest man in Ire,' said Obierika.

'You are right,' Ofoedu agreed. 'But you ought to ask why the drum has not been beaten to tell Umuofia of his death.'

'Why?' asked Obierika and Okonkwo together.

'That is the strange part of it. You know his first wife who walks with a stick?'

'Yes. She is called Ozoemena.'

'That is so,' said Ofoedu. 'Ozoemena was, as you know, too old to attend Ndulue during his illness. His younger wives did that. When he died this morning, one of these women went to Ozoemena's hut and told her. She rose from her mat, took her stick and walked over to the *obi*. She knelt on her knees and hands at the threshold and called her husband, who was laid on a mat. "Ogbuefi Ndulue," she called, three times, and went back to her hut. When the youngest wife went to call her again to be present at the washing of the body, she found her lying on the mat, dead.'

'That is very strange indeed,' said Okonkwo. 'They will put off Ndulue's funeral until his wife has been buried.'

'That is why the drum has not been beaten to tell Umuofia.'

'It was always said the Ndulue and Ozoemena had one mind,' said

Obierika. 'I remember when I was a young boy there was a song about them. He could not do anything without telling her.'

'I did not know that,' said Okonkwo. 'I thought he was a strong man in his youth.'

'He was indeed,' said Ofoedu.

Okonkwo shook his head doubtfully.

'He led Umuofia to war in those days,' said Obierika.

◆

Okonkwo was beginning to feel like his old self again. All that he required was something to occupy his mind. If he had killed Ikemefuna during the busy planting season or harvesting it would not have been so bad; his mind would have been centred on his work. Okonkwo was not a man of thought but of action. But in the absence of work, talking was the next best.

Soon after Ofoedu left, Okonkwo took up his goatskin bag to go.

'I must go home to tap my palm trees for the afternoon,' he said.

'Who taps your tall trees for you?' asked Obierika.

'Umezulike,' replied Okonkwo.

'Sometimes I wish I had not taken the *ozo* title,' said Obierika. 'It wounds my heart to see these young men killing palm trees in the name of tapping.'

'It is so indeed,' Okonkwo agreed. 'But the law of the land must be obeyed.'

'I don't know how we got that law,' said Obierika. 'In many other clans a man of title is not forbidden to climb the palm tree. Here we say he cannot climb the tall tree but he can tap the short ones standing on the ground. It is like Dimaragana, who would not lend his knife for cutting up dog-meat because the dog was taboo to him, but offered to use his teeth.'

'I think it is good that our clan holds the *ozo* title in high esteem,' said Okonkwo. 'In those other clans you speak of, *ozo* is so low that every beggar takes it.'

'I was only speaking in jest,' said Obierika. 'In Abame and Aninta the title is worth less than two cowries. Every man wears the thread of title on his ankle, and does not lose it even if he steals.'

'They have indeed soiled the name of *ozo*,' said Okonkwo as he rose to go.

'It will not be very long now before my in-laws come,' said Obierika.

'I shall return very soon,' said Okonkwo, looking at the position of the sun.

◆

There were seven men in Obierika's hut when Okonkwo returned. The suitor was a young man of about twenty-five, and with him were his father and uncle. On Obierika's side were his two elder brothers and Maduka, his sixteen-year-old son.

'Ask Akueke's mother to send us some kola nuts,' said Obierika to his son. Maduka vanished into the compound like lightning. The conversation at once centred on him, and everybody agreed that he was as sharp as a razor.

'I sometimes think he is too sharp,' said Obierika, somewhat indulgently. 'He hardly ever walks. He is always in a hurry. If you are sending him on an errand he flies away before he has heard half of the message.'

'You were very much like that yourself,' said his eldest brother. 'As our people say, "When mother-cow is chewing grass its young ones watch its mouth." Maduka has been watching your mouth.'

As he was speaking the boy returned, followed by Akueke, his half-sister, carrying a wooden dish with three kola nuts and alligator pepper. She gave the dish to her father's eldest brother and then shook hands, very shyly, with her suitor and his relatives. She was about sixteen and just ripe for marriage. Her suitor and his relatives surveyed her young body with expert eyes as if to assure themselves that she was beautiful and ripe.

She wore a coiffure which was done up into a crest in the middle of the head. Cam wood was rubbed lightly into her skin, and all over her body were black patterns drawn with *uli*. She wore a black necklace which hung down in three coils just above her full, succulent breasts. On her arms were red and yellow bangles, and on her waist four or five rows of *jigida*, or waist-beads.

When she had shaken hands, or rather held out her hand to be shaken, she returned to her mother's hut to help with the cooking.

'Remove your *jigida* first,' her mother warned as she moved near the fireplace to bring the pestle resting against the wall. 'Every day I tell you that *jigida* and fire are not friends. But you will never hear. You grew your ears for decoration, not for hearing. One of these days your *jigida* will catch fire on your waist, and then you will know.'

Akueke moved to the other end of the hut and began to remove the waist-beads. It had to be done slowly and carefully, taking each string separately, else it would break and the thousand tiny rings would have to be strung together again. She rubbed each string downwards with her palms until it passed the buttocks and slipped down to the floor around her feet.

The men in the *obi* had already begun to drink the palm-wine which Akueke's suitor had brought. It was a very good wine and powerful, for in spite of the palm fruit hung across the mouth of the pot to restrain the lively liquor, white foam rose and spilled over.

'That wine is the work of a good tapper,' said Okonkwo.

The young suitor, whose name was Ibe, smiled broadly and said to his father: 'Do you hear that?' He then said to the others: 'He will never admit that I am a good tapper.'

'He tapped three of my best palm trees to death,' said his father, Ukegbu.

'That was about five years ago,' said Ibe, who had begun to pour out the wine, 'before I learnt how to tap.' He filled the first horn and gave it to his father. Then he poured out for the others. Okonkwo brought out his big horn from the goatskin bag, blew into it to remove any dust that might be there, and gave it to Ibe to fill.

As the men drank, they talked about everything except the thing for which they had gathered. It was only after the pot had been emptied that the suitor's father cleared his voice and announced the object of their visit.

Obidrika then presented to him a small bundle of short broomsticks. Ukegbu counted them.

'They are thirty?' he asked.

Obierika nodded in agreement.

'We are at last getting somewhere,' Ukegbu said, and then turning to his brother and his son he said: 'Let us go out and whisper together.' The three rose and went outside. When they returned Ukegbu handed the bundle of sticks back to Obierika. He counted them; instead of thirty there were now only fifteen. He passed them over to his eldest brother, Machi, who also counted them and said:

'We had not thought to go below thirty. But as the dog said, "If I fall down for you and you fall down for me, it is play". Marriage should be a play and not a fight; so we are falling down again.' He then added ten sticks to the fifteen and gave the bundle to Ukegbu.

In this way Akueke's bride-price was finally settled at twenty bags of cowries. It was already dusk when the two parties came to this agreement.

'Go and tell Akueke's mother that we have finished,' Obierika said to his son, Maduka. Almost immediately the woman came in with a big bowl of foo-foo. Obierika's second wife followed with a pot of soup, and Maduka brought in a pot of palm-wine.

As the men ate and drank palm-wine they talked about the customs of their neighbours.

'It was only this morning,' said Obierika, 'that Okonkwo and I were talking about Abame and Aninta, where titled men climb trees and pound foo-foo for their wives.'

'All their customs are upside-down. They do not decide bride-price as we do, with sticks. They haggle and bargain as if they were buying a goat or a cow in the market.'

'That is very bad,' said Obierika's eldest brother. 'But what is good in one place is bad in another place. In Umunso they do not bargain at all, not even with broomsticks. The suitor just goes on bringing bags of cowries until his in-laws tell him to stop. It is a bad custom because it always leads to a quarrel.'

'The world is large,' said Okonkwo. 'I have even heard that in some tribes a man's children belong to his wife and her family.'

'That cannot be,' said Machi. 'You might as well say that the woman lies on top of the man when they are making the children.'

'It is like the story of white men who, they say, are white like this piece of chalk,' said Obierika. He held up a piece of chalk, which every man kept in his *obi* and with which his guests drew lines on the

51

floor before they ate kola nuts. 'And these white men, they say, have no toes.'

'And have you never seen them?' asked Machi.

'Have you?' asked Obierika.

'One of them passes here frequently,' said Machi. 'His name is Amadi.'

Those who knew Amadi laughed. He was a leper, and the polite name for leprosy was 'the white skin'.

Chapter Nine

For the first time in three nights, Okonkwo slept. He woke up once in the middle of the night and his mind went back to the past three days without making him feel uneasy. He began to wonder why he had felt uneasy at all. It was like a man wondering in broad daylight why a dream had appeared so terrible to him at night. He stretched himself and scratched his thigh where a mosquito had bitten him as he slept. Another one was wailing near his right ear. He slapped the ear and hoped he had killed it. Why do they always go for one's ears? When he was a child his mother had told him a story about it. But it was as silly as all women's stories. Mosquito, she had said, had asked Ear to marry him, whereupon Ear fell on the floor in uncontrollable laughter. 'How much longer do you think you will live?' she asked. 'You are already a skeleton.' Mosquito went away humiliated, and any time he passed her way he told Ear that he was still alive.

Okonkwo turned on his side and went back to sleep. He was roused in the morning by someone banging on his door.

'Who is that?' he growled. He knew it must be Ekwefi. Of his three wives Ekwefi was the only one who would have the audacity to bang on his door.

'Ezinma is dying,' came her voice, and all the tragedy and sorrow of her life were packed in those words.

Okonkwo sprang from his bed, pushed back the bolt on his door and ran into Ekwefi's hut.

Ezinma lay shivering on a mat beside a huge fire that her mother had kept burning all night.

'It is *iba*,' said Okonkwo as he took his matchet and went into the bush to collect the leaves and grasses and barks of trees that went into making the medicine for *iba*.

53

Ekwefi knelt beside the sick child, occasionally feeling with her palm the wet, burning forehead.

Ezinma was an only child and the centre of her mother's world. Very often it was Ezinma who had decided what food her mother should prepare. Ekwefi even gave her such delicacies as eggs, which children were rarely allowed to eat because such food tempted them to steal. One day as Ezinma was eating an egg Okonkwo had come in unexpectedly from his hut. He was greatly shocked and swore to beat Ekwefi if she dared to give the child eggs again. But it was impossible to refuse Ezinma anything. After her father's rebuke she developed an even keener appetite for eggs. And she enjoyed above all the secrecy in which she now ate them. Her mother always took her into their bedroom and shut the door.

Ezinma did not call her mother *Nne* like all children. She called her by her name, Ekwefi, as her father and other grown-up people did. The relationship between them was not only that of mother and child. There was something in it like the companionship of equals, which was strengthened by such little conspiracies as eating eggs in the bedroom.

Ekwefi had suffered a good deal in her life. She had borne ten children and nine of them had died in infancy, usually before the age of three. As she buried one child after another her sorrow gave way to despair and then to grim resignation. The birth of her children, which should be a woman's crowning glory, became for Ekwefi mere physical agony devoid of promise. The naming ceremony after seven market weeks became an empty ritual. Her deepening despair found expression in the names she gave her children. One of them was a pathetic cry, Onwumbiko – 'Death, I implore you.' But Death took no notice; Onwumbiko died in his fifteenth month. The next child was a girl, Ozoemena – 'May it not happen again.' She died in her eleventh month, and two others after her. Ekwefi then became defiant and called her next child Onwuma – 'Death may please himself.' And he did.

After the death of Ekwefi's second child, Okonkwo had gone to a medicine-man, who was also a diviner of the Afa Oracle, to inquire what was amiss. This man told him that the child was an *ogbanje*, one

54

of those wicked children who, when they died, entered their mother's womb to be born again.

'When your wife becomes pregnant again,' he said, 'let her not sleep in her hut. Let her go and stay with her people. In that way she will elude her wicked tormentor and break its evil cycle of birth and death.'

Ekwefi did as she was asked. As soon as she became pregnant she went to live with her old mother in another village. It was there that her third child was born and circumcised on the eighth day. She did not return to Okonkwo's compound until three days before the naming ceremony. The child was called Onwumbiko.

Onwumbiko was not given proper burial when he died. Onkonkwo had called in another medicine-man who was famous in the clan for his great knowledge about *ogbanje* children. His name was Okagbue Uyanwa. Okagbue was a very striking figure, tall, with a full beard and a bald head. He was light in complexion and his eyes were red and fiery. He always gnashed his teeth as he listened to those who came to consult him. He asked Okonkwo a few questions about the dead child. All the neighbours and relations who had come to mourn gathered round them.

'On what market-day was it born?' he asked.

'*Oye,*' replied Okonkwo.

'And it died this morning?'

Okonkwo said yes, and only then realised for the first time that the child had died on the same market-day as it had been born. The neighbours and relations also saw the coincidence and said among themselves that it was very significant.

'Where do you sleep with your wife, in your *obi* or in her own hut?' asked the medicine-man.

'In her hut.'

'In future call her into your *obi*.'

The medicine-man then ordered that there should be no mourning for the dead child. He brought out a sharp razor from the goatskin bag slung from his left shoulder and began to mutilate the child. Then he took it away to bury in the Evil Forest, holding it by the ankle and dragging it on the ground behind him. After such treatment it would think twice before coming again, unless it was one of the stubborn

55

ones who returned, carrying the stamp of their mutilation – a missing finger or perhaps a dark line where the medicine-man's razor had cut them.

By the time Onwumbiko died Ekwefi had become a very bitter woman. Her husband's first wife had already had three sons, all strong and healthy. When she had borne her third son in succession, Okonkwo had slaughtered a goat for her, as was the custom. Ekwefi had nothing but good wishes for her. But she had grown so bitter about her own *chi* that she could not rejoice with others over their good fortune. And so, on the day that Nwoye's mother celebrated the birth of her three sons with feasting and music, Ekwefi was the only person in the happy company who went about with a cloud on her brow. Her husband's wife took this for malevolence, as husbands' wives were wont to. How could she know that Ekwefi's bitterness did not flow outwards to others but inwards into her own soul; that she did not blame others for their good fortune but her own evil *chi* who denied her any?

At last Ezinma was born, and although ailing she seemed determined to live. At first Ekwefi accepted her, as she had accepted others – with listless resignation. But when she lived on to her fourth, fifth and sixth years, love returned once more to her mother, and, with love, anxiety. She determined to nurse her child to health, and she put all her being into it. She was rewarded by occasional spells of health during which Ezinma bubbled with energy like fresh palm-wine. At such times she seemed beyond danger. But all of a sudden she would go down again. Everybody knew she was an *ogbanje*. These sudden bouts of sickness and health were typical of her kind. But she had lived so long that perhaps she had decided to stay. Some of them did become tired of their evil rounds of birth and death, or took pity on their mothers, and stayed. Ekwefi believed deep inside her that Ezinma had come to stay. She believed because it was that faith alone that gave her own life any kind of meaning. And this faith had been strengthened when a year or so ago a medicine-man had dug up Ezinma's *iyi-uwa*. Everyone knew then that she would live because her bond with the world of *ogbanje* had been broken. Ekwefi was reassured. But such was her anxiety for her daughter that she could not rid herself completely of her fear. And although she believed that the *iyi-uwa* which had been dug up was genuine, she could not ignore the fact that some really evil children sometimes misled people into digging up a specious one.

But Ezinma's *iyi-uwa* had looked real enough. It was a smooth pebble wrapped in a dirty rag. The man who dug it up was the same Okagbue who was famous in all the clan for his knowledge in these matters. Ezinma had not wanted to co-operate with him at first. But that was only to be expected. No *ogbanje* would yield her secrets easily, and most of them never did because they died too young – before they could be asked questions.

'Where did you bury your *iyi-uwa*?' she asked in return.

'You know where it is. You buried it in the ground somewhere so that you can die and return again to torment your mother.'

Ezinma looked at her mother, whose eyes, sad and pleading, were fixed on her.

'Answer the question at once,' roared Okonkwo, who stood beside her. All the family were there and some of the neighbours too.

'Leave her to me,' the medicine-man told Okonkwo in a cool, confident voice. He turned again to Ezinma. 'Where did you bury your *iyi-uwa*?'

'Where they bury children,' she replied, and the quiet spectators murmured to themselves.

'Come along then and show me the spot,' said the medicine-man.

The crowd set out with Ezinma leading the way and Okagbue following closely behind her. Okonkwo came next and Ekwefi followed him. When she came to the main road, Ezinma turned left as if she was going to the stream.

'But you said it was where they bury children?' asked the medicine-man.

'No,' said Ezinma, whose feeling of importance was manifest in her sprightly walk. She sometimes broke into a run and stopped again suddenly. The crowd followed her silently. Women and children returning from the stream with pots of water on their heads wondered what was happening until they saw Okagbue and guessed that it must be something to do with *ogbanje*. And they all knew Ekwefi and her daughter very well.

When she got to the big udala tree Ezinma turned left into the bush, and the crowd followed her. Because of her size she made her way through trees and creepers more quickly than her followers. The bush was alive with the tread of feet on dry leaves and sticks and the moving aside of tree branches. Ezinma went deeper and deeper and the crowd went with her. Then she suddenly turned round and began to walk back to the road. Everybody stood to let her pass and then filed after her.

'If you bring us all this way for nothing I shall beat sense into you,' Okonkwo threatened.

'I have told you to let her alone. I know how to deal with them,' said Okagbue.

Ezinma led the way back to the road, looked left and right and turned right. And so they arrived home again.

'Where did you bury your *iyi-uwa*?' asked Okagbue when Ezinma finally stopped outside her father's *obi*. Okagbue's voice was unchanged. It was quiet and confident.

'It is near that orange tree,' Ezinma said.

'And why did you not say so, you wicked daughter of Akalogoli?' Okonkwo swore furiously. The medicine-man ignored him.

'Come and show me the exact spot,' he said quietly to Ezinma.

'It is here,' she said when they got to the tree.

'Point at the spot with your finger,' said Okagbue.

'It is here,' said Ezinma touching the ground with her finger. Okonkwo stood by, rumbling like thunder in the rainy season.

'Bring me a hoe,' said Okagbue.

When Ekwefi brought the hoe, he had already put aside his goatskin bag and his big cloth and was in his underwear, a long and thin strip of cloth wound round the waist like a belt and then passed between the legs to be fastened to the belt behind. He immediately set to work digging a pit where Ezinma had indicated. The neighbours sat around watching the pit becoming deeper and deeper. The dark top-soil soon gave way to the bright-red earth with which women scrubbed the floor and walls of huts. Okagbue worked tirelessly and in silence, his back shining with perspiration. Okonkwo stood by the pit. He asked Okagbue to come up and rest while he took a hand. But Okagbue said he was not tired yet.

Ekwefi went into her hut to cook yams. Her husband had brought out more yams than usual because the medicine-man had to be fed. Ezinma went with her and helped in preparing the vegetables.

'There is too much green vegetable,' she said.

'Don't you see the pot is full of yams?' Ekwefi asked. 'And you know how leaves become smaller after cooking.'

'Yes,' said Ezinma, 'that was why the snake-lizard killed his mother.'

'Very true,' said Ekwefi.

'He gave his mother seven baskets of vegetables to cook and in the end there were only three. And so he killed her,' said Ezinma.

'That is not the end of the story.'

'Oho,' said Ezinma, 'I remember now. He brought another seven baskets and cooked them himself. And there were again only three. So he killed himself too.'

Outside the *obi* Okagbue and Okonkwo were digging the pit to find where Ezinma had buried her *iyi-uwa*. Neighbours sat around, watching. The pit was now so deep that they no longer saw the digger. They only saw the red earth he threw up mounting higher and higher. Okonkwo's son, Nwoye, stood near the edge of the pit because he wanted to take in all that happened.

Okagbue had again taken over the digging from Okonkwo. He worked, as usual, in silence. The neigbours and Okonkwo's wives were now talking. The children had lost interest and were playing.

Suddenly Okagbue sprang to the surface with the agility of a leopard.

'It is very near now,' he said. 'I have felt it.'

There was immediate excitement and those who were sitting jumped to their feet.

'Call your wife and child,' he said to Okonkwo. But Ekwefi and Ezinma had heard the noise and run out to see what it was.

Okagbue went back into the pit, which was now surrounded by spectators. After a few more hoe-fuls of earth he struck the *iyi-uwa*. He raised it carefully with the hoe and threw it to the surface. Some women ran away in fear when it was thrown. But they soon returned and everyone was gazing at the rag from a reasonable distance. Okagbue emerged and without saying a word or even looking at the spectators he went to his goatskin bag, took out two leaves and began to chew them. When he had swallowed them, he took up the rag with his left hand and began to untie it. And then the smooth, shiny pebble fell out. He picked it up.

'Is this yours?' he asked Ezinma.

'Yes,' she replied. All the women shouted with joy because Ekwefi's troubles were at last ended.

All this had happened more than a year ago and Ezinma had not been ill since. And then suddenly she had begun to shiver in the night. Ekwefi brought her to the fireplace, spread her mat on the floor and built a fire. But she had got worse and worse. As she knelt by her, feeling with her palm the wet, burning forehead, she prayed a thousand times. Although her husband's wives were saying that it was nothing more than *iba*, she did not hear them.

◆

Okonkwo returned from the bush carrying on his left shoulder a large bundle of grasses and leaves, roots and barks of medicinal trees and shrubs. He went into Ekwefi's hut, put down his load and sat down.

'Get me a pot,' he said, 'and leave the child alone.'

Ekwefi went to bring the pot and Okonkwo selected the best from his bundle, in their due proportion, and cut them up. He put them in the pot and Ekwefi poured in some water.

'Is that enough?' she asked when she had poured in about half of the water in the bowl.

'A little more . . . I said a *little*. Are you deaf?' Okonkwo roared at her.

She set the pot on the fire and Okonkwo took up his matchet to return to his *obi*.

'You must watch the pot carefully,' he said as he went, 'and don't allow it to boil over. If it does its power will be gone.' He went away to his hut and Ekwefi began to tend the medicine pot almost as if it was itself a sick child. Her eyes went constantly from Ezinma to the boiling pot and back to Ezinma.

Okonkwo returned when he felt the medicine had cooked long enough. He looked it over and said it was done.

'Bring a low stool for Ezinma,' he said, 'and a thick mat.'

He took down the pot from the fire and placed it in front of the stool. He then roused Ezinma and placed her on the stool, astride the steaming pot. The thick mat was thrown over both. Ezinma struggled to escape from the choking and overpowering steam, but she was held down. She started to cry.

When the mat was at last removed she was drenched in perspiration. Ekwefi mopped her with a piece of cloth and she lay down on a dry mat and was soon asleep.

Chapter Ten

Large crowds began to gather on the village *ilo* as soon as the edge had worn off the sun's heat and it was no longer painful on the body. Most communal ceremonies took place at that time of the day, so that even when it was said that a ceremony would begin 'after the midday meal' everyone understood that it would begin a long time later, when the sun's heat had softened.

It was clear from the way the crowd stood or sat that the ceremony was for men. There were many women, but they looked on from the fringe like outsiders. The titled men and elders sat on their stools waiting for the trials to begin. In front of them was a row of stools on which nobody sat. There were nine of them. Two little groups of people stood at a respectable distance beyond the stools. They faced the elders. There were three men in one group and three men and one woman in the other. The woman was Mgbafo and the three men with her were her brothers. In the other group were her husband, Uzowulu, and his relatives. Mgbafo and her brothers were as still as statues into whose faces the artist has moulded defiance. Uzowulu and his relatives, on the other hand, were whispering together. It looked like whispering, but they were really talking at the top of their voices. Everybody in the crowd was talking. It was like the market. From a distance the noise was a deep rumble carried by the wind.

An iron gong sounded, setting up a wave of expectation in the crowd. Everyone looked in the direction of the *egwugwu* house. *Gome, gome, gome, gome* went the gong, and a powerful flute blew a high-pitched blast. Then came the voices of the *egwugwu*, gutteral and awesome. The wave struck the women and children and there was a backward stampede. But it was momentary. They were already far enough where they stood and there was room for running away if any of the *egwugwu* should go towards them.

The drum sounded again and the flute blew. The *egwugwu* house was now a pandemonium of quavering voices: *Aru oyim de de de dei!* filled the air as the spirits of the ancestors, just emerged from the earth, greeted themselves in their esoteric language. The *egwugwu* house into which they emerged faced the forest, away from the crowd, who saw only its back with the many-coloured patterns and drawings done by specially chosen women at regular intervals. These women never saw the inside of the hut. No woman ever did. They scrubbed and painted the outside walls under the supervision of men. If they imagined what was inside, they kept their imagination to themselves. No woman ever asked questions about the most powerful and the most secret cult in the clan.

Aru oyim de de de dei! flew around the dark, closed hut like tongues of fire. The ancestral spirits of the clan were abroad. The metal gong beat continuously now and the flute, shrill and powerful, floated on the chaos.

And then the *egwugwu* appeared. The women and children sent up a great shout and took to their heels. It was instinctive. A woman fled as soon as an *egwugwu* came in sight. And when, as on that day, nine of the greatest masked spirits in the clan came out together it was a terrifying spectacle. Even Mgbafo took to her heels and had to be restrained by her brothers.

Each of the nine *egwugwu* represented a village of the clan. Their leader was called Evil Forest. Smoke poured out of his head.

The nine villages of Umuofia had grown out of the nine sons of the first father of the clan. Evil Forest represented the village of Umeru, or the children of Eru, who was the eldest of the nine sons.

'*Umuofia kwenu!*' shouted the leading *egwugwu*, pushing the air with his raffia arms. The elders of the clan replied, '*Yao!*'

'*Umuofia kwenu!*'

'*Yaa!*'

'*Umuofia kwenu!*'

'*Yaa!*'

Evil Forest then thrust the pointed end of his rattling staff into the earth. And it began to shake and rattle, like something agitating with a metallic life. He took the first of the empty stools and the eight other *egwugwu* began to sit in order of seniority after him.

Okonkwo's wives, and perhaps other women as well, might have noticed that the second *egwugwu* had the springy walk of Okonkwo. And they might also have noticed that Okonkwo was not among the titled men and elders who sat behind the row of *egwugwu*. But if they thought these things they kept them within themselves. The *egwugwu* with the springy walk was one of the dead fathers of the clan. He looked terrible with the smoked raffia body, a huge wooden face painted white except for the round hollow eyes and the charred teeth that were as big as a man's fingers. On his head were two powerful horns.

When all the *egwugwu* had sat down and the sound of the many tiny bells and rattles on their bodies had subsided, Evil Forest addressed the two groups of people facing them.

'Uzowulu's body, I salute you,' he said. Spirits always addressed humans as 'bodies'. Uzowulu bent down and touched the earth with his right hand as a sign of submission.

'Our father, my hand has touched the ground,' he said.

'Uzowulu's body, do you know me?' asked the spirit.

'How can I know you, father? You are beyond our knowledge.'

Evil Forest then turned to the other group and addressed the eldest of the three brothers.

'The body of Odukwe, I greet you,' he said, and Odukwe bent down and touched the earth. The hearing then began.

Uzowulu stepped forward and presented his case.

'That woman standing there is my wife, Mgbafo. I married her with my money and my yams. I do not owe my in-laws anything. I owe them no yams. I owe them no coco-yams. One morning three of them came to my house, beat me up and took my wife and children away. This happened in the rainy season. I have waited in vain for my wife to return. At last I went to my in-laws and said to them, "You have taken back your sister. I did not send her away. You yourselves took her. The law of the clan is that you should return her bride-price." But my wife's brother said they had nothing to tell me. So I have brought the matter to the fathers of the clan. My case is finished. I salute you.'

'Your words are good,' said the leader of the *egwugwu*. 'Let us hear Odukwe. His words may also be good.'

Odukwe was short and thick-set. He stepped forward, saluted the spirits and began his story.

'My in-law has told you that we went to his house, beat him up and took our sister and her children away. All that is true. He told you that he came to take back her bride-price and we refused to give it him. That is also true. My in-law, Uzowulu, is a beast. My sister lived with him for nine years. During those years no single day passed in the sky without his beating the woman. We have tried to settle their quarrels time without number and on each occasion Uzowulu was guilty – '

'It is a lie!' Uzowulu shouted.

'Two years ago,' continued Odukwe, 'when she was pregnant, he beat her until she miscarried.'

'It is a lie. She miscarried after she had gone to sleep with her lover.'

'Uzowulu's body, I salute you,' said Evil Forest, silencing him. 'What kind of lover sleeps with a pregnant woman?' There was a loud murmur of approbation from the crowd. Odukwe continued:

'Last year when my sister was recovering from an illness, he beat her again so that if the neighbours had not gone in to save her she would have been killed. We heard of it, and did as you have been told. The law of Umuofia is that if a woman runs away from her husband her bride-price is returned. But in this case she ran away to save her life. Her two children belong to Uzowulu. We do not dispute it, but they are too young to leave their mother. If, on the other hand, Uzowulu should recover from his madness and come in the proper way to beg his wife to return she will do so on the understanding that if he ever beats her again we shall cut off his genitals for him.'

The crowd roared with laughter. Evil Forest rose to his feet and order was immediately restored. A steady cloud of smoke rose from his head. He sat down again and called two witnesses. They were both Uzowulu's neighbours, and they agreed about the beating. Evil Forest then stood up, pulled out his staff and thrust it into the earth again. He ran a few steps in the direction of the women; they all fled in terror, only to return to their places almost immediately. The nine *egwugwu* then went away to consult together in their house. They were silent for a long time. Then the metal gong sounded and the flute was blown. The *egwugwu* had emerged once again from their underground home. They saluted one another and then reappeared on the *ilo*.

'*Umuofia kwenu!*' roared Evil Forest, facing the elders and grandees of the clan.

'*Yaa!*' replied the thunderous crowd, then silence descended from the sky and swallowed the noise.

Evil Forest began to speak and all the while he spoke everyone was silent. The eight other *egwugwu* were as still as statues.

'We have heard both sides of the case,' said Evil Forest. 'Our duty is not to blame this man or to praise that, but to settle the dispute.' He turned to Uzowulu's group and allowed a short pause.

'Uzowulu's body, do you know me?'

'How can I know you, father? You are beyond our knowledge,' Uzowulu replied.

'I am Evil Forest. I kill a man on the day that his life is sweetest to him.'

'That is true,' replied Uzowulu.

'Go to your in-laws with a pot of wine and beg your wife to return to you. It is not bravery when a man fights with a woman.' He turned to Odukwe, and allowed a brief pause.

'Odukwe's body, I greet you,' he said.

'My hand is on the ground,' replied Odukwe.

'Do you know me?'

'No man can know you,' replied Odukwe.

'I am Evil Forest, I am Dry-meat-that-fills-the-mouth, I am Fire-that-burns-without-faggots. If your in-law brings wine to you, let your sister go with him. I salute you.' He pulled his staff from the hard earth and thrust it back.

'*Umuofia kwenu!*' he roared, and the crowd answered.

'I don't know why such a trifle should come before the *egwugwu*,' said one elder to another.

'Don't you know what kind of man Uzowulu is? He will not listen to any other decision,' replied the other.

As they spoke two other groups of people had replaced the first before the *egwugwu*, and a great land case began.

Chapter Eleven

The night was impenetrably dark. The moon had been rising later and later every night until now it was seen only at dawn. And whenever the moon forsook evening and rose at cock-crow the nights were as black as charcoal.

Ezinma and her mother sat on a mat on the floor after their supper of yam foo-foo and bitter leaf soup. A palm-oil lamp gave out yellowish light. Without it, it would have been impossible to eat; one could not have known where one's mouth was in the darkness of that night. There was an oil lamp in all four huts on Okonkwo's compound, and each hut seen from the others looked like a soft eye of yellow half-light set in the solid massiveness of night.

The world was silent except for the shrill cry of insects, which was part of the night, and the sound of wooden mortar and pestle as Nwayieke pounded her foo-foo. Nwayieke lived four compounds away, and she was notorious for her late cooking. Every woman in the neighbourhood knew the sound of Nwayieke's mortar and pestle. It was also part of the night.

Okonkwo had eaten from this wives' dishes and was now reclining with his back against the wall. He searched his bag and brought out his snuff-bottle. He turned it on to his left palm, but nothing came out. He hit the bottle against his knee to shake up the tobacco. That was always the trouble with Okeke's snuff. It very quickly went damp, and there was too much saltpetre in it. Okonkwo had not brought snuff from him for a long time. Idigo was the man who knew how to grind good snuff. But he had recently fallen ill.

Low voices, broken now and again by singing, reached Okonkwo from his wives' huts as each woman and her children told folk stories. Ekwefi and her daughter, Ezinma, sat on a mat on the floor. It was Ekwefi's turn to tell a story.

'Once upon a time,' she began, 'all the birds were invited to a feast in the sky. They were very happy and began to prepare themselves for the great day. They painted their bodies with red cam wood and drew beautiful patterns on them with *uli*.

'Tortoise saw all these preparations and soon discovered what it all meant. Nothing that happened in the world of the animals ever escaped his notice; he was full of cunning. As soon as he heard of the great feast in the sky his throat began to itch at the very thought. There was a famine in those days and Tortoise had not eaten a good meal for two moons. His body rattled like a piece of dry stick in his empty shell. So he began to plan how he would go to the sky.'

'But he had no wings,' said Ezinma.

'Be patient,' replied her mother. 'That is the story. Tortoise had no wings, but he went to the birds and asked to be allowed to go with them.

'"We know you too well," said the birds when they had heard him. "You are full of cunning and you are ungrateful. If we allow you to come with us you will soon begin your mischief."

'"You do not know me," said Tortoise. "I am a changed man. I have learnt that a man who makes trouble for others is also making it for himself."

'Tortoise had a sweet tongue, and within a short time all the birds agreed that he was a changed man, and they each gave him a feather, with which he made two wings.

'At last the great day came and Tortoise was the first to arrive at the meeting-place. When all the birds had gathered together, they set off in a body. Tortoise was very happy and voluble as he flew among the birds, and he was soon chosen as the man to speak for the party because he was a great orator.

'"There is one important thing which we must not forget," he said as they flew on their way. "When people are invited to a great feast like this, they take new names for the occasion. Our hosts in the sky will expect us to honour this age-old custom."

'None of the birds had heard of this custom but they knew that Tortoise, in spite of his failings in other directions, was a widely-travelled man who knew the customs of different people. And so they each took a new name. When they had all taken, Tortoise also took one. He was to be called *All of you*.

'At last the party arrived in the sky and their hosts were very happy to see them. Tortoise stood up in his many-coloured plumage and thanked them for their invitation. His speech was so eloquent that all the birds were glad they had brought him, and nodded their heads in approval of all he said. Their hosts took him as the king of the birds, especially as he looked somewhat different from the others.

'After kola nuts had been presented and eaten, the people of the sky set before their guests the most delectable dishes Tortoise had ever seen or dreamt of. The soup was brought out hot from the fire and in the very pot in which it had been cooked. It was full of meat and fish. Tortoise began to sniff aloud. There was pounded yam and also yam pottage cooked with palm-oil and fresh fish. There were also pots of palm-wine. When everything had been set before the guests, one of the people of the sky came forward and tasted a little from each pot. He then invited the birds to eat. But Tortoise jumped to his feet and asked: "For whom have you prepared this feast?"

'"For all of you," replied the man.

'Tortoise turned to the birds and said: "You remember that my name is *All of you*. The custom here is to serve the spokesman first and the others later. They will serve you when I have eaten."

'He began to eat and the birds grumbled angrily. The people of the sky thought it must be their custom to leave all the food for their king. And so Tortoise ate the best part of the food and then drank two pots of palm-wine, so that he was full of food and drink and his body filled out in his shell.

'The birds gathered round to eat what was left and to peck at the bones he had thrown all about the floor. Some of them were too angry to eat. They chose to fly home on an empty stomach. But before they left each took back the feather he had lent to Tortoise. And there he stood in his hard shell full of food and wine but without any wings to fly home. He asked the birds to take a message for his wife, but they all refused. In the end Parrot, who had felt more angry than the others, suddenly changed his mind and agreed to take the message.

'"Tell my wife," said Tortoise, "to bring out all the soft things in my house and cover the compound with them so that I can jump down from the sky without very great danger."

'Parrot promised to deliver the message, and then flew away. But when he reached Tortoise's house he told his wife to bring out all the hard things in the house. And so she brought out her husband's hoes, matchets, spears, guns and even his cannon. Tortoise looked down from the sky and saw his wife bringing things out, but it was too far to see what they were. When all seemed ready he let himself go. He fell and fell and fell until he began to fear that he would never stop falling. And then like the sound of his cannon he crashed on the compound.'

'Did he die?' asked Ezinma.

'No,' replied Ekwefi. 'His shell broke into pieces. But there was a great medicine-man in the neigbourhood. Tortoise's wife sent for him and he gathered all the bits of shell and stuck them together. That is why Tortoise's shell is not smooth.'

'There is no song in the story,' Ezinma pointed out.

'No,' said Ekwefi. 'I shall think of another one with a song. But it is your turn now.'

'Once upon a time,' Ezinma began, 'Tortoise and Cat went to wrestle against Yams – no, that is not the beginning. Once upon a time there was a great famine in the land of animals. Everybody was lean except Cat, who was fat and whose body shone as if oil was rubbed on it . . .'

She broke off because at that very moment a loud and high-pitched voice broke the outer silence of the night. It was Chielo, the priestess of Agbala, prophesying. There was nothing new in that. Once in a while Chielo was possessed by the spirit of her god and she began to prophesy. But tonight she was addressing her prophecy and greetings to Okonkwo, and so everyone in his family listened. The folk stories stopped.

'Agbala do-o-o-o! Agbala ekeneo-o-o-o,' came the voice like a sharp knife cutting through the night. 'Okonkwo! Agbala ekene gio-o-o-o! Agbala cholu ifu ada ya Ezinmao-o-o-o!'

At the mention of Ezinma's name Ekwefi jerked her head sharply like a animal that had sniffed death in the air. Her heart jumped painfully within her.

The priestess had now reached Okonkwo's compound and was talking with him outside his hut. She was saying again and again that Agbala wanted to see his daughter, Ezinma. Okonkwo pleaded with her to come back in the morning because Ezinma was now asleep. But Chielo ignored what he was trying to say and went on shouting that Agbala wanted to see his daughter. Her voice was as clear as metal, and Okonkwo's women and children heard from their huts all that she said. Okonkwo was still pleading that the girl had been ill of late and was asleep. Ekwefi quickly took her to their bedroom and placed her on their high bamboo bed.

The priestess suddenly screamed. 'Beware, Okonkwo!' she warned. 'Beware of exchanging words with Agbala. Does a man speak when a god speaks? Beware!'

She walked through Okonkwo's hut into the circular compound and went straight towards Ekwefi's hut. Okonkwo came after her.

'Ekwefi,' she called, 'Agbala greets you. Where is my daughter, Ezinma? Agbala wants to see her.'

Ekwefi came out from her hut carrying her oil lamp in her left hand. There was a light wind blowing, so she cupped her right hand to shelter the flame. Nwoye's mother, also carrying an oil lamp, emerged from her hut. Her children stood in the darkness outside their hut watching the strange event. Okonkwo's youngest wife also came out and joined the others.

'Where does Agbala want to see her?' Ekwefi asked.

'Where else but in his house in the hills and the caves?' replied the priestess.

'I will come with you, too,' Ekwefi said firmly.

'Tufia-a!' the priestess cursed, her voice cracking like the angry bark of thunder in the dry season. 'How dare you, woman, to go before the mighty Agbala of your own accord? Beware, woman, lest he strike you in his anger. Bring me my daughter.'

Ekwefi went into her hut and came out again with Ezinma.

'Come, my daughter,' said the priestess. 'I shall carry you on my back. A baby on its mother's back does not know that the way is long.'

Ezinma began to cry. She was used to Chielo calling her 'my

daughter'. But it was a different Chielo she now saw in the yellow half-light.

'Don't cry, my daughter,' said the priestess, 'lest Agbala be angry with you.'

'Don't cry,' said Ekwefi, 'she will bring you back very soon. I shall give you some fish to eat.' She went into the hut again and brought down the smoke-black basket in which she kept her dried fish and other ingredients for cooking soup. She broke a piece in two and gave it to Ezinma, who clung to her.

'Don't be afraid,' said Ekwefi, stroking her head, which was shaved in places, leaving a regular pattern of hair. They went outside again. The priestess bent down on one knee and Ezinma climbed on her back, her left palm closed on her fish and her eyes gleaming with tears.

'*Agbala do-o-o-o! Agbala ekeneo-o-o-o-o!* . . .' Chielo began once again to chant greetings to her god. She turned round sharply and walked through Okonkwo's hut, bending very low at the eaves. Ezinma was crying loudly now, calling on her mother. The two voices disappeared into the thick darkness.

A strange and sudden weakness descended on Ekwefi as she stood gazing in the direction of the voices like a hen whose only chick has been carried away by a kite. Ezinma's voice soon faded away and only Chielo was heard moving farther and farther into the distance.

'Why do you stand there as though she had been kidnapped?' asked Okonkwo as he went back to his hut.

'She will bring her back soon,' Nwoye's mother said.

But Ekwefi did not hear these consolations. She stood for a while, and then, all of a sudden, made up her mind. She hurried through Okonkwo's hut and went outside.

'Where are you going?' he asked.

'I am following Chielo,' she replied and disappeared in the darkness. Okonkwo cleared his throat, and brought out his snuff-bottle from the goatskin bag by his side.

◆

The priestess's voice was already growing faint in the distance. Ekwefi hurried to the main footpath and turned left in the direction of the voice. Her eyes were useless to her in the darkness. But she picked her way easily on the sandy footpath hedged on either side by branches and damp leaves. She began to run, holding her breasts with her hands to stop them flapping noisily against her body. She hit her left foot againt an outcropped root, and terror seized her. It was an ill omen. She ran faster. But Chielo's voice was still a long way away. Had she been running too? How could she go so fast with Ezinma on her back? Although the night was cool, Ekwefi was beginning to feel hot from her running. She continually ran into the luxuriant weeds and creepers that walled in the path. Once she tripped up and fell. Only then did she realise, with a start, that Chielo had stopped her chanting. Her heart beat violently and she stood still. Then Chielo's renewed outburst came from only a few paces ahead. But Ekwefi could not see her. She shut her eyes for a while and opened them again in an effort to see. But it was useless. She could not see beyond her nose.

There were no stars in the sky because there was a rain-cloud. Fireflies went about with their tiny green lamps, which only made the darkness more profound. Between Chielo's outbursts the night was alive with the shrill tremor of forest insects woven into the darkness.

'*Agbala do-o-o-o! ... Agbala ekeneo-o-o-o! ...*' Ekwefi trudged behind, neither getting too near nor keeping too far back. She thought they must be going towards the sacred cave. Now that she walked slowly she had time to think. What would she do when they got to the cave? She would not dare to enter. She would wait at the mouth, all alone in that fearful place. She thought of all the terrors of the night. She remembered the night, long ago, when she had seen *Ogbu-agali-odu*, one of those evil essences loosed upon the world by the potent 'medicines' which the tribe had made in the distant past against its enemies but had now forgotten how to control. Ekwefi had been returning from the stream with her mother on a dark night like this when they saw its glow as it flew in their direction. They had thrown their water-pots and lain by the roadside expecting the sinister light to descend on them and kill them. That was the only time Ekwefi ever saw *Ogbu-agali-odu*. But although it had happened so long ago, her blood still ran cold whenever she remembered that night.

The priestess's voice came at longer intervals now, but its vigour was undiminished. The air was cool and damp with dew. Ezinma sneezed. Ekwefi muttered, 'Life to you.' At the same time the priestess also said, 'Life to you, my daughter.' Ezinma's voice from the darkness warmed her mother's heart. She trudged slowly along.

And then the priestess screamed. 'Somebody is walking behind me!' she said. 'Whether you are spirit or man, may Agbala shave your head with a blunt razor! May he twist your neck until you see your heels!'

Ekwefi stood rooted to the spot. One mind said to her: 'Woman, go home before Agbala does you harm.' But she could not. She stood until Chielo had increased the distance between them and she began to follow again. She had already walked so long that she began to feel a slight numbness in the limbs and in the head. Then it occurred to her that they could not have been heading for the cave. They must have by-passed it long ago; they must be going towards Umuachi, the farthest village in the clan. Chielo's voice now came after long intervals.

It seemed to Ekwefi that the night had become a little lighter. The cloud had lifted and a few stars were out. The moon must be preparing to rise, its sullenness over. When the moon rose later in the night, people said it was refusing food, as a sullen husband refuses his wife's food when they have quarrelled.

'*Agbala do-o-o-o! Umuachi! Agbala ekene unuo-o-o!*' It was just as Ekwefi had thought. The priestess was now saluting the village of Umuachi. It was unbelievable, the distance they had covered. As they emerged into the open village from the narrow forest track the darkness was softened and it became possible to see the vague shape of trees. Ekwefi screwed her eyes up in an effort to see her daughter and the priestess, but whenever she thought she saw their shape it immediately dissolved like a melting lump of darkness. She walked numbly along.

Chielo's voice was now rising continuously, as when she first set out. Ekwefi had a feeling of spacious openness, and she guessed they must be on the village *ilo*, or playground. And she realised too with something like a jerk that Chielo was no longer moving forward. She was, in fact, returning. Ekwefi quickly moved away from her line of retreat. Chielo passed by, and they began to go back the way they had come.

It was a long and weary journey and Ekwefi felt like a sleepwalker most of the way. The moon was definitely rising, and although it had not yet appeared on the sky its light had already melted down the darkness. Ekwefi could now discern the figure of the priestess and her burden. She slowed down her pace so as to increase the distance between them. She was afraid of what might happen if Chielo suddenly turned round and saw her.

She had prayed for the moon to rise. But now she found the half-light of the incipient moon more terrifying than the darkness. The world was now peopled with vague, fantastic figures that dissolved under her steady gaze and then formed again in new shapes. At one stage Ekwefi was so afraid that she nearly called out to Chielo for companionship and human sympathy. What she had seen was the shape of a man climbing a palm tree, his head pointing to the earth and his legs skywards. But at that very moment Chielo's voice rose again in her possessed chanting, and Ekwefi recoiled, because there was no humanity there. It was not the same Chielo who sat with her in the market and sometimes bought bean-cakes for Ezinma, whom she called her daughter. It was a different woman – the priestess of Agbala, the Oracle of the Hills and Caves. Ekwefi trudged along between two fears. The sound of her benumbed steps seemed to come from some other person walking behind her. Her arms were folded across her bare breasts. Dew fell heavily and the air was cold. She could no longer think, not even about the terrors of night. She just jogged along in a half-sleep only waking to full life when Chielo sang.

At last they took a turning and began to head for the caves. From then on, Chielo never ceased in her chanting. She greeted her god in a multitude of names – the owner of the future, the messenger of earth, the god who cut a man down when his life was sweetest to him. Ekwefi was also awakened and her benumbed fears revived.

The moon was now up and she could see Chielo and Ezinma clearly. How a woman could carry a child of that size so easily and for so long was a miracle. But Ekwefi was not thinking about that. Chielo was not a woman that night.

'*Agbala do-o-o-o! Agbala ekeneo-o-o! Chi negbu madu ubosi ndu ya nato ya uto daluo-o-o! . . .*'

Ekwefi could already see the hills looming in the moonlight. They formed a circular ring with a break at one point through which the foot-track led to the centre of the circle.

As soon as the priestess stepped into this ring of hills her voice was not only doubled in strength but was thrown back on all sides. It was indeed the shrine of a great god. Ekwefi picked her way carefully and quietly. She was already beginning to doubt the wisdom of her coming. Nothing would happen to Ezinma, she thought. And if anything happened to her could she stop it? She would not dare to enter the underground caves. Her coming was quite useless, she thought.

As these things went through her mind she did not realise how close they were to the cave mouth. And so when the priestess with Ezinma on her back disappeared through a hole hardly big enough to pass a hen, Ekwefi broke into a run as though to stop them. As she stood gazing at the circular darkness which had swallowed them, tears gushed from her eyes, and she swore within her that if she heard Ezinma cry she would rush into the cave to defend her against all the gods in the world. She would die with her.

Having sworn that oath, she sat down on a stony ledge and waited. Her fear had vanished. She could hear the priestess's voice, all its metal taken out of it by the vast emptiness of the cave. She buried her face in her lap and waited.

She did not know how long she waited. It must have been a very long time. Her back was turned on the footpath that led out of the hills. She must have heard a noise behind her and turned round sharply. A man stood there with a matchet in his hand. Ekwefi uttered a scream and sprang to her feet.

'Don't be foolish,' said Okonkwo's voice. 'I thought you were going into the shrine with Chielo,' he mocked.

Ekwefi did not answer. Tears of gratitude filled her eyes. She knew her daughter was safe.

'Go home and sleep,' said Okonkwo. 'I shall wait here.'

'I shall wait too. It is almost dawn. The first cock has crowed.'

As they stood there together, Ekwefi's mind went back to the days when they were young. She had married Anene because Okonkwo

76

was too poor then to marry. Two years after her marriage to Anene she could bear it no longer and she ran away to Okonkwo. It had been early in the morning. The moon was shining. She was going to the stream to fetch water. Okonkwo's house was on the way to the stream. She went in and knocked at his door and he came out. Even in those days he was not a man of many words. He just carried her into his bed and in the darkness began to feel around her waist for the loose end of her cloth.

Chapter Twelve

On the following morning the entire neighbourhood wore a festive air because Okonkwo's friend, Obierika, was celebrating his daughter's *uri*. It was the day on which her suitor (having already paid the greater part of her bride-price) would bring palm-wine not only to her parents and immediate relatives but to the wide and extensive group of kinsmen called *umunna*. Everybody had been invited – men, women and children. But it was really a woman's ceremony and the central figures were the bride and her mother.

As soon as day broke, breakfast was hastily eaten and women and children began to gather at Obierika's compound to help the bride's mother in her difficult but happy task of cooking for a whole village.

Okonkwo's family was astir like any other family in the neighbourhood. Nwoye's mother and Okonkwo's youngest wife were ready to set out for Obierika's compound with all their children. Nwoye's mother carried a basket of coco-yams, a cake of salt and smoked fish which she would present to Obierika's wife. Okonkwo's youngest wife, Ojiugo, also had a basket of plantains and coco-yams and a small pot of palm-oil. Their children carried pots of water.

Ekwefi was tired and sleepy from the exhausting experiences of the previous night. It was not very long since they had returned. The priestess, with Ezinma sleeping on her back, had crawled out of the shrine on her belly like a snake. She had not as much as looked at Okonkwo and Ekwefi or shown any surprise at finding them at the mouth of the cave. She looked straight ahead of her and walked back to the village. Okonkwo and his wife followed at a respectful distance. They thought the priestess might be going to her house, but she went to Okonkwo's compound, passed through his *obi* and into Ekwefi's hut and walked into her bedroom. She placed Ezinma carefully on the bed and went away without saying a word to anybody.

Ezinma was still sleeping when everyone else was astir, and Ekwefi asked Nwoye's mother and Ojiugo to explain to Obierika's wife that she would be late. She had got ready her basket of coco-yams and fish, but she must wait for Ezinma to wake.

'You need some sleep yourself,' said Nwoye's mother. 'You look very tired.'

As they spoke Ezinma emerged from the hut, rubbing her eyes and stretching her spare frame. She saw the other children with their water-pots and remembered that they were going to fetch water for Obierika's wife. She went back to the hut and brought her pot.

'Have you slept enough?' asked her mother.

'Yes,' she replied. 'Let us go.'

'Not before you have had your breakfast,' said Ekwefi. And she went into her hut to warm the vegetable soup she had cooked last night.

'We shall be going,' said Nwoye's mother. 'I will tell Obierika's wife that you are coming later.' And so they all went to help Obierika's wife – Nwoye's mother and her four children and Ojiugo with her two.

As they trooped through Okonkwo's *obi* he asked: 'Who will prepare my afternoon meal?'

'I shall return to do it,' said Ojiugo.

Okonkwo was also feeling tired and sleepy, for although nobody else knew it, he had not slept at all last night. He had felt very anxious but did not show it. When Ekwefi had followed the priestess, he had allowed what he regarded as a reasonable and manly interval to pass and then gone with his matchet to the shrine, where he thought they must be. It was only when he had got there that it had occurred to him that the priestess might have chosen to go round the villages first. Okonkwo had returned home and sat waiting. When he thought he had waited long enough he again returned to the shrine. But the Hills and the Caves were as silent as death. It was only on his fourth trip that he had found Ekwefi, and by then he had become gravely worried.

◆

Obierika's compound was as busy as an ant-hill. Temporary cooking tripods were erected on every available space by bringing together three blocks of sun-dried earth and making a fire in their midst. Cooking pots went up and down the tripods, and foo-foo was pounded in a hundred wooden mortars. Some of the women cooked the yams and the cassava, the others prepared vegetable soup. Young men pounded the foo-foo or split firewood. The children made endless trips to the stream.

Three young men helped Obierika to slaughter the two goats with which the soup was made. They were very fat goats, but the fattest of all was tethered to a peg near the wall of the compound. It was as big as a small cow. Obierika had sent one of his relatives all the way to Umuike to buy that goat. It was the one he would present alive to his in-laws.

'The market of Umuike is a wonderful place,' said the young man who had been sent by Obierika to buy the giant goat. 'There are so many people on it that if you threw up a grain of sand it would not find a way to fall to earth again.'

'It is the result of a great medicine,' said Obierika. 'The people of Umuike wanted their market to grow and swallow up the markets of their neighbours. So they made a powerful medicine. Every market-day, before the first cock-crow, this medicine stands on the market-ground in the shape of an old woman with a fan. With this magic fan she beckons to the market all the neighbouring clans. She beckons in front of her and behind her, to her right and to her left.'

'And so everybody comes,' said another man, 'honest men and thieves. They can steal your cloth from off your waist in that market.'

'Yes,' said Obierika. 'I warned Nwankwo to keep a sharp eye and a sharp ear. There was once a man who went to sell a goat. He led it on a thick rope which he tied round his wrist. But as he walked through the market he realised that people were pointing at him as they do to a madman. He could not understand it until he looked back and saw that what he led at the end of the tether was not a goat but a heavy log of wood.'

'Do you think a thief can do that kind of thing single-handed?' asked Nwankwo.

'No,' said Obierika. 'They use medicine.'

When they had cut the goats' throats and collected the blood in a bowl, they held them over an open fire to burn off the hair, and the smell of burning hair blended with the smell of cooking. Then they washed them and cut them up for the women who prepared the soup.

All this ant-hill activity was going smoothly when a sudden interruption came. It was a cry in the distance: *Oji odu achu iiiji-o-o!* (*The one that uses its tail to drive flies away!*) Every woman immediately abandoned whatever she was doing and rushed out in the direction of the cry.

'We cannot all rush out like that, leaving what we are cooking to burn in the fire,' shouted Chielo, the priestess. 'Three or four of us should stay behind.'

'It is true,' said another woman. 'We will allow three or four women to stay behind.'

Five women stayed behind to look after the cooking-pots, and all the rest rushed away to see the cow that had been let loose. When they saw it they drove it back to its owner, who at once paid the heavy fine which the village imposed on anyone whose cow was let loose on his neighbours' crops. When the women had exacted the penalty they checked among themselves to see if any woman had failed to come out when the cry had been raised.

'Where is Mgbogo?' asked one of them.

'She is ill in bed,' said Mgbogo's next-door neighbour. 'She has *iba*.'

'The only other person is Udenkwo,' said another woman, 'and her child is not twenty-eight days yet.'

Those women whom Obierika's wife had not asked to help her with the cooking returned to their homes, and the rest went back, in a body, to Obierika's compound.

'Whose cow is it?' asked the women who had been allowed to stay behind.

'It was my husband's,' said Ezelagbo. 'One of the young children had opened the gate of the cow-shed.'

◆

Early in the afternoon the first two pots of palm-wine arrived from Obierika's in-laws. They were duly presented to the women, who drank a cup or two each, to help them in their cooking. Some of it also went to the bride and her attendant maidens, who were putting the last delicate touches of razor to her coiffure and cam wood on her smooth skin.

When the heat of the sun began to soften, Obierika's son, Maduka, took a long broom and swept the ground in front of his father's *obi*. And as if they had been waiting for that, Obierika's relatives and friends began to arrive, every man with his goatskin bag hung on one shoulder and a rolled goatskin mat under his arm. Some of them were accompanied by their sons bearing carved wooden stools. Okonkwo was one of them. They sat in a half circle and began to talk of many things. It would not be long before the suitors came.

Okonkwo brought out his snuff-bottle and offered it to Ogbuefi Ezenwa, who sat next to him. Ezenwa took it, tapped it on his knee-cap, rubbed his left palm on his body to dry it before tipping a little snuff into it. His actions were deliberate, and he spoke as he performed them.

'I hope our in-laws will bring many pots of wine. Although they come from a village that is known for being close-fisted, they ought to know that Akueke is the bride for a king.'

'They dare not bring fewer than thirty pots,' said Okonkwo. 'I shall tell them my mind if they do.'

At that moment Obierika's son, Maduka, led out the giant goat from the inner compound, for his father's relatives to see. They all admired it and said that that was the way things should be done. The goat was then led back to the inner compound.

Very soon after, the in-laws began to arrive. Young men and boys in single file, each carrying a pot of wine, came first. Obierika's relatives counted the pots as they came. Twenty, twenty-five. There was a long break, and the hosts looked at each other as if to say, 'I told you.' Then more pots came. Thirty, thirty-five, forty, forty-five. The hosts nodded in approval and seemed to say, 'Now they are behaving like men.' Altogether there were fifty pots of wine. After the pot-bearers came Ibe, the suitor, and the elders of his family. They sat in a half-moon, thus completing a circle with their hosts. The pots of wine stood in their midst. Then the bride, her mother and half a dozen other women and girls emerged from the inner compound, and went round the circle shaking hands with all. The bride's mother led the way, followed by the bride and the other women. The married women wore their best cloths and the girls wore red and black waist-beads and anklets of brass.

When the women retired. Obierika presented kola nuts to his in-laws. His eldest brother broke the first one. 'Life to all of us,' he said as he broke it. 'And let there be friendship between your family and ours.'

The crowd answered: '*Ee-e-e!*'

'We are giving you our daughter today. She will be a good wife to you. She will bear you nine sons like the mother of our town.'

'*Ee-e-e!*'

The oldest man in the camp of the visitors replied: 'It will be good for you and it will be good for us.'

'*Ee-e-e!*'

'This is not the first time my people have come to marry your daughter. My mother was one of you.'

'*Ee-e-e!*'

'And this will not be the last, because you understand us and we understand you. You are a great family.'

'*Ee-e-e!*'

'Prosperous men and great warriors.' He looked in the direction of Okonkwo. 'Your daughter will bear us sons like you.'

'*Ee-e-e!*'

The kola was eaten and the drinking of palm-wine began. Groups of four or five men sat round with a pot in their midst. As the evening wore on, food was presented to the guests. There were huge bowls of foo-foo and steaming pots of soup. There were also pots of yam pottage. It was a great feast.

◆

As night fell, burning torches were set on wooden tripods and the young men raised a song. The elders sat in a circle and the singers went round singing each man's praise as they came before him. They had something to say for every man. Some were great farmers, some were orators who spoke for the clan; Okonkwo was the greatest wrestler and warrior alive. When they had gone round the circle they settled down in the centre, and girls came from the inner compound to dance. At first the bride was not among them. But when she finally appeared holding a cock in her right hand, a loud cheer rose from the crowd. All the other dancers made way for her. She presented the cock to the musicians and began to dance. Her brass anklets rattled as she danced and her body gleamed with cam wood in the soft yellow light. The musicians with their wood, clay and metal instruments went from song to song. And they were all gay. They sang the latest song in the village:

> 'If I hold her hand
>   She says, "Don't touch!"
> If I hold her foot
>   She says, "Don't touch!"
> But when I hold her waist beads
>   She pretends not to know.'

The night was already far spent when the guests rose to go, taking their bride home to spend seven market weeks with her suitor's family. They sang songs as they went, and on their way they paid short courtesy visits to prominent men like Okonkwo, before they finally left for their village. Okonkwo made a present of two cocks to them.

Chapter Thirteen

Go-di-di-go-go-di-go. Di-go-go-di-go. It was the *ekwe* talking to the clan. One of the things every man learned was the language of the hollowed-out instrument. Diim! Diim! Diim! boomed the cannon at intervals.

The first cock had not crowed, and Umuofia was still swallowed up in sleep and silence when the *ekwe* began to talk, and the cannon shattered the silence. Men stirred on their bamboo beds and listened anxiously. Somebody was dead. The cannon seemed to rend the sky. Di-go-go-di-go-di-di-go-go floated in the message-laden night air. The faint and distant wailing of women settled like a sediment of sorrow on the earth. Now and again a full-chested lamentation rose above the wailing whenever a man came into the place of death. He raised his voice once or twice in manly sorrow and then sat down with the other men listening to the endless wailing of the women and the esoteric language of the *ekwe*. Now and again the cannon boomed. The wailing of the women would not be heard beyond the village, but the *ekwe* carried the news to all the nine villages and even beyond. It began by naming the clan: *Umuofia obodo dike* 'the land of the brave.' *Umuofia obodo dike! Umuofia obodo dike!* It said this over and over again, and as it dwelt on it, anxiety mounted in every heart that heaved on a bamboo bed that night. Then it went nearer and named the village: *Iguedo of the yellow grinding-stone!* It was Okonkwo's village. Again and again Iguedo was called and men waited breathlessly in all the nine villages. At last the man was named and people sighed 'E-u-u, Ezeudu is dead.' A cold shiver ran down Okonkwo's back as he remembered the last time the old man had visited him. 'That boy calls you father,' he had said. 'Bear no hand in his death.'

◆

Ezeudu was a great man, and so all the clan was at his funeral. The ancient drums of death beat, guns and cannon were fired, and men dashed about in frenzy, cutting down every tree or animal they saw, jumping over walls and dancing on the roof. It was a warrior's funeral, and from morning till night warriors came and went in their age-groups. They all wore smoked raffia skirts and their bodies were painted with chalk and charcoal. Now and again an ancestral spirit or *egwugwu* appeared from the underworld, speaking in a tremulous, unearthly voice and completely covered in raffia. Some of them were very violent, and there had been a mad rush for shelter earlier in the day when one appeared with a sharp matchet and was only prevented from doing serious harm by two men who restrained him with the help of a strong rope tied round his waist. Sometimes he turned round and chased those men, and they ran for their lives. But they always returned to the long rope he trailed behind. He sang, in a terrifying voice, that Ekwenzu, or Evil Spirit, had entered his eye.

But the most dreaded of all was yet to come. He was always alone and was shaped like a coffin. A sickly odour hung in the air wherever he went, and flies went with him. Even the greatest medicine-men took shelter when he was near. Many years ago another *egwugwu* had dared to stand his ground before him and had been transfixed to the spot for two days. This one had only one hand and with it carried a basket full of water.

But some of the *egwugwu* were quite harmless. One of them was so old and infirm that he leaned heavily on a stick. He walked unsteadily to the place where the corpse was laid, gazed at it a while and went away again – to the underworld.

The land of the living was not far removed from the domain of the ancestors. There was coming and going between them, especially at festivals and also when an old man died, because an old man was very close to the ancestors. A man's life from birth to death was a series of transition rites which brought him nearer and nearer to his ancestors.

Ezeudu had been the oldest man in the village, and at his death there were only three men in the whole clan who were older, and four or five others in his own age-group. Whenever one of these ancient men appeared in the crowd to dance unsteadily the funeral steps of the tribe, younger men gave way and the tumult subsided.

It was a great funeral, such as befitted a noble warrior. As the evening drew near, the shouting and the firing of guns, the beating of drums and the brandishing and clanging of matchets increased.

Ezeudu had taken three titles in his life. It was a rare achievement. There were only four titles in the clan, and only one or two men in any generation ever achieved the fourth and highest. When they did, they became the lords of the land. Because he had taken titles, Ezeudu was to be buried after dark with only a glowing brand to light the sacred ceremony.

But before this quiet and final rite, the tumult increased tenfold. Drums beat violently and men leaped up and down in a frenzy. Guns were fired on all sides and sparks flew out as matchets clanged together in warriors' salutes. The air was full of dust and the smell of gunpowder. It was then that the one-handed spirit came, carrying a basket full of water. People made way for him on all sides and the noise subsided. Even the smell of gunpowder was swallowed in the sickly smell that now filled the air. He danced a few steps to the funeral drums and then went to see the corpse.

'Ezeudu!' he called in his gutteral voice. 'If you had been poor in your last life I would have asked you to be rich when you come again. But you were rich. If you had been a coward, I would have asked you to bring courage. But you were a fearless warrior. If you had died young, I would have asked you to get life. But you lived long. So I shall ask you to come again the way you came before. If your death was the death of nature, go in peace. But if a man caused it, do not allow him a moment's rest.' He danced a few more steps and went away.

◆

The drums and the dancing began again and reached fever-heat. Darkness was around the corner, and the burial was near. Guns fired the last salute and the cannon rent the sky. And then from the centre of the delirious fury came a cry of agony and shouts of horror. It was as if a spell had been cast. All was silent. In the centre of the crowd a boy lay in a pool of blood. It was the dead man's sixteen-year-old son, who with his brothers and half-brothers had been dancing the traditional farewell to their father. Okonkwo's gun had exploded and a piece of iron had pierced the boy's heart.

The confusion that followed was without parallel in the tradition of Umuofia. Violent deaths were frequent, but nothing like this had ever happened.

The only course open to Okonkwo was to flee from the clan. It was a crime against the earth goddess to kill a clansman, and a man who committed it must flee from the land. The crime was of two kinds, male and female. Okonkwo had committed the female, because it had been inadvertent. He could return to the clan after seven years.

That night he collected his most valuable belongings into headloads. His wives wept bitterly and their children wept with them without knowing why. Obierika and half a dozen other friends came to help and to console him. They each made nine or ten trips carrying Okonkwo's yams to store in Obierika's barn. And before the cock crowed Okonkwo and his family were fleeing to his motherland. It was a little village called Mbanta, just beyond the borders of Mbaino.

As soon as the day broke, a large crowd of men from Ezeudu's quarter stormed Okonkwo's compound, dressed in garbs of war. They set fire to his houses, demolished his red walls, killed his animals and destroyed his barn. It was the justice of the earth goddess, and they were merely her messengers. They had no hatred in their hearts against Okonkwo. His greatest friend, Obierika, was among them. They were merely cleansing the land which Okonkwo had polluted with the blood of a clansman.

Obierika was a man who thought about things. When the will of the goddess had been done, he sat down in his *obi* and mourned his friend's calamity. Why should a man suffer so greviously for an offence he had committed inadvertently? But although he thought for a long time he found no answer. He was merely led into greater complexities. He remembered his wife's twin children, whom he had thrown away. What crime had they committed? The Earth had decreed that they were an offence on the land and must be destroyed. And if the clan did not exact punishment for an offence against the great goddess, her wrath was loosed on all the land and not just on the offender. As the elders said, if one finger brought oil it soiled the others.

PART TWO

Chapter Fourteen

Okonkwo was well received by his mother's kinsmen in Mbanta. The old man who received him was his mother's younger brother, who was now the eldest surviving member of that family. His name was Uchendu, and it was he who had received Okonkwo's mother twenty and ten years before when she had been brought home from Umuofia to be buried with her people. Okonkwo was only a boy then and Uchendu still remembered him crying the traditional farewell: 'Mother, mother, mother is going.'

That was many years ago. Today Okonkwo was not bringing his mother home to be buried with her people. He was taking his family of three wives and eleven children to seek refuge in his motherland. As soon as Uchendu saw him with his sad and weary company he guessed what had happened, and asked no questions. It was not until the following day that Okonkwo told him the full story. The old man listened silently to the end and then said with some relief: 'It is a female *ochu*.' And he arranged the requisite rites and sacrifices.

Okonkwo was given a plot of ground on which to build his compound, and two or three pieces of land on which to farm during the coming planting season. With the help of his mother's kinsmen he built himself an *obi* and three huts for his wives. He then installed his personal god and the symbols of his departed fathers. Each of Uchendu's five sons contributed three hundred seed-yams to enable their cousin to plant a farm, for as soon as the first rain came farming would begin.

At last the rain came. It was sudden and tremendous. For two or three moons the sun had been gathering strength till it seemed to breathe a breath of fire on the earth. All the grass had long been scorched brown, and the sand felt like live coals to the feet. Evergreen trees wore a dusty coat of brown. The birds were silenced in the forests,

ay panting under the live, vibrating heat. And then came
of thunder. It was an angry, metallic and thirsty clap, unlike
e deep and liquid rumbling of the rainy season. A mighty wind arose
and filled the air with dust. Palm trees swayed as the wind combed
their leaves into flying crests like strange and fantastic coiffure.

When the rain finally came, it was in large, solid drops of frozen
water which the people called 'the nuts of the water of heaven'. They
were hard and painful on the body as they fell, yet young people ran
about happily picking up the cold nuts and throwing them into their
mouths to melt.

The earth quickly came to life and the birds in the forests fluttered
around and chirped merrily. A vague scent of life and green vegetation
was diffused in the air. As the rain began to fall more soberly and in
smaller liquid drops, children sought for shelter, and all were happy,
refreshed and thankful.

◆

Okonkwo and his family worked very hard to plant a new farm. But
it was like beginning life anew without the vigour and enthusiasm of
youth, like learning to become left-handed in old age. Work no longer
had for him the pleasure it used to have, and when there was no work
to do he sat in a silent half-sleep.

His life had been ruled by a great passion – to become one of the
lords of the clan. That had been his life-spring. And he had all but
achieved it. Then everything had been broken. He had been cast out
of his clan like a fish on to a dry, sandy beach, panting. Clearly his
personal god or *chi* was not made for great things. A man could not
rise beyond the destiny of his *chi*. The saying of the elders was not
true – that if a man said yea his *chi* also affirmed. Here was a man
whose *chi* said nay despite his own affirmation.

The old man, Uchendu, saw clearly that Okonkwo had yielded to
despair and he was greatly troubled. He would speak to him after the
isa-ifi ceremony.

◆

The youngest of Uchendu's five sons, Amikwu, was marrying a new wife. The bride-price had been paid and all but the last ceremony had been performed. Amikwu and his people had taken palm-wine to the bride's kinsmen about two moons before Okonkwo's arrival in Mbanta. And so it was time for the final ceremony of confession.

The daughters of the family were all there, some of them having come a long way from their homes in distant villages. Uchendu's eldest daughter had come from Obodo, nearly half a day's journey away. The daughters of Uchendu's brothers were also there. It was a full gathering of *umuada*, in the same way as they would meet if a death occurred in the family. There were twenty-two of them.

They sat in a big circle on the ground and the bride sat in the centre with a hen in her right hand. Uchendu sat by her, holding the ancestral staff of the family. All the other men stood outside the circle, watching. Their wives watched also. It was evening and the sun was setting.

Uchendu's eldest daughter, Njide, asked the questions.

'Remember that if you do not answer truthfully you will suffer or even die at child-birth,' she began. 'How many men have lain with you since my brother first expressed the desire to marry you?'

'None,' she replied simply.

'Answer truthfully,' urged the other women.

'None?' asked Njide.

'None,' she answered.

'Swear on this staff of my fathers,' said Uchendu.

'I swear,' said the bride.

Uchendu took the hen from her, slit its throat with a sharp knife and allowed some of the blood to fall on his ancestral staff.

From that day Amikwu took the young bride to his hut and she became his wife. The daughters of the family did not return to their homes immediately but spent two or three days with their kinsmen.

◆

On the second day Uchendu called together his sons and daughters and his nephew, Okonkwo. The men brought their goatskin mats, with which they sat on the floor, and the women sat on a sisal mat spread on a raised bank of earth. Uchendu pulled gently at his grey beard and gnashed his teeth. Then he began to speak, quietly and deliberately, picking his words with great care:

'It is Okonkwo that I primarily wish to speak to,' he began. 'But I want all of you to note what I am going to say. I am an old man and you are all children. I know more about the world than any of you. If there is any one among you who thinks he knows more let him speak up.' He paused, but no one spoke.

'Why is Okonkwo with us today? This is not his clan. We are only his mother's kinsmen. He does not belong here. He is an exile, condemned for seven years to live in a strange land. And so he is bowed with grief. But there is just one question I would like to ask him. Can you tell me, Okonkwo, why it is that one of the commonest names we give our children is Nneka, or "Mother is Supreme?" We all know that a man is the head of the family and his wives do his bidding. A child belongs to its father and his family and not to its mother and her family. A man belongs to his fatherland and not to his motherland. And yet we say Nneka – "Mother is Supreme". Why is that?'

There was silence. 'I want Okonkwo to answer me,' said Uchendu.

'I do not know the answer,' Okonkwo replied.

'You do not know the answer? So you see that you are a child. You have many wives and many children – more children than I have. You are a great man in your clan. But you are still a child, *my* child. Listen to me and I shall tell you. But there is one more question I shall ask. Why is it that when a woman dies she is taken home to be buried with her own kinsmen? She is not buried with her husband's kinsmen. Why is that? Your mother was brought home to me and buried with my people. Why was that?'

Okonkwo shook his head.

'He does not know that either,' said Uchendu, 'and yet he is full of sorrow because he has come to live in his motherland for a few years.' He laughed a mirthless laughter, and turned to his sons and daughters. 'What about you? Can you answer my question?'

They all shook their heads.

'Then listen to me,' he said and cleared his throat. 'It's true that a child belongs to its father. But when a father beats his child, it seeks sympathy in its mother's hut. A man belongs to his fatherland when

94

things are good and life is sweet. But when there is sorrow and bitterness he finds refuge in his motherland. Your mother is there to protect you. She is buried there. And that is why we say that mother is supreme. Is it right that you, Okonkwo, should bring your mother a heavy face and refuse to be comforted? Be careful or you may displease the dead. Your duty is to comfort your wives and children and take them back to your fatherland after seven years. But if you allow sorrow to weigh you down and kill you, they will all die in exile.' He paused for a long while. 'These are now your kinsmen.' He waved at his sons and daughters. 'You think you are the greatest sufferer in the world. Do you know that men are sometimes banished for life? Do you know that men sometimes lose all their yams and even their children? I had six wives once. I have none now except that young girl who knows not her right from her left. Do you know how many children I have buried – children I begot in my youth and strength? Twenty-two. I did not hang myself, and I am still alive. If you think you are the greatest sufferer in the world ask my daughter, Akeuni, how many twins she has borne and thrown away. Have you not heard the song they sing when a woman dies?

> ' "For whom is it well, for whom is it well?
> There is no one for whom it is well."

'I have no more to say to you.'

Chapter Fifteen

It was in the second year of Okonkwo's exile that his friend, Obierika, came to visit him. He brought with him two young men, each of them carrying a heavy bag on his head. Okonkwo helped them put down their loads. It was clear that the bags were full of cowries.

Okonkwo was very happy to receive his friend. His wives and children were very happy too, and so were his cousins and their wives when he sent for them and told them who his guest was.

'You must take him to salute our father,' said one of the cousins.

'Yes,' replied Okonkwo. 'We are going directly.' But before they went he whispered something to his first wife. She nodded, and soon the children were chasing one of their cocks.

Uchendu had been told by one of his grandchildren that three strangers had come to Okonkwo's house. He was therefore waiting to receive them. He held out his hands to them when they came into his *obi*, and after they had shaken hands he asked Okonkwo who they were.

'This is Obierika, my great friend. I have already spoken to you about him.'

'Yes,' said the old man, turning to Obierika. 'My son has told me about you, and I am happy you have come to see us. I knew your father, Iweka. He was a great man. He had many friends here and came to see them quite often. Those were good days when a man had friends in distant clans. Your generation does not know that. You stay at home, afraid of your next-door neighbour. Even a man's mother-land is strange to him nowadays.' He looked at Okonkwo. 'I am an old man and I like to talk. That is all I am good for now.' He got up painfully, went into an inner room and came back with a kola nut.

'Who are the young men with you?' he asked as he sat down again on his goatskin. Okonkwo told him.

'Ah,' he said. 'Welcome, my sons.' He presented the kola nut to them, and when they had seen it and thanked him, he broke it and they ate.

'Go into that room,' he aid to Okonkwo, pointing with his finger. 'You will find a pot of wine there.'

Okonkwo brought the wine and they began to drink. It was a day old, and very strong.

'Yes,' said Uchendu after a long silence. 'People travelled more in those days. There is not a single clan in these parts that I do not know very well. Aninta, Umuazu, Ikeocha, Elumelu, Abame – I know them all.'

'Have you heard,' asked Obierika, 'that Abame is no more?'

'How is that?' asked Uchendu and Okonkwo together.

'Abame has been wiped out,' said Obierika. 'It is a strange and terrible story. If I had not seen the few survivors with my own eyes and heard their story with my own ears, I would not have believed. Was it not on an Eke day that they fled into Umuofia?' he asked his two companions, and they nodded their heads.

'Three moons ago,' said Obierika, 'on an Eke market-day a little band of fugitives came into our town. Most of them were sons of our land whose mothers had been buried with us. But there were some too who came because they had friends in our town, and others who could think of nowhere else open to escape. And so they fled into Umuofia with a woeful story.' He drank his palm-wine, and Okonkwo filled his horn again. He continued:

'During the last planting season a white man had appeared in their clan.'

'An albino,' suggested Okonkwo.

'He was not an albino. He was quite different.' He sipped his wine. 'And he was riding an iron horse. The first people who saw him ran away, but he stood beckoning to them. In the end the fearless ones were near and even touched him. The elders consulted their Oracle and it told them that the strange man would break their clan and spread destruction among them.' Obierika again drank a little of his wine. 'And so they killed the white man and tied his iron horse to their sacred tree because it looked as if it would run away to call the man's friends. I forgot to tell you another thing which the Oracle said.

97

It said that other white men were on their way. They were locusts, it said, and that first man was their harbinger sent to explore the terrain. And so they killed him.'

'What did the white man say before they killed him?' asked Uchendu.

'He said nothing,' answered one of Obierika's companions.

'He said something, only they did not understand him,' said Obierika. 'He seemed to speak through his nose.'

'One of the men told me,' said Obierika's other companion, 'that he repeated over and over again a word that resembled Mbaino. Perhaps he had been going to Mbaino and had lost his way.'

'Anyway,' resumed Obierika, 'they killed him and tied up his iron horse. This was before the planting season began. For a long time nothing happened. The rains had come and yams had been sown. The iron horse was still tied to the sacred silk-cotton tree. And then one morning three white men led by a band of ordinary men like us came to the clan. They saw the iron horse and went away again. Most of the men and women of Abame had gone to their farms. Only a few of them saw these white men and their followers. For many market weeks nothing else happened. They have a big market in Abame on every other Afo day and, as you know, the whole clan gathers there. That was the day it happened. The three white men and a very large number of other men surrounded the market. They must have used a powerful medicine to make themselves invisible until the market was full. And they began to shoot. Everybody was killed, except the old and the sick who were at home and a handful of men and women whose *chi* were wide awake and brought them out of that market.' He paused.

'Their clan is now completely empty. Even the sacred fish in their mysterious lake have fled and the lake has turned the colour of blood. A great evil has come upon their land as the Oracle had warned.'

There was a long silence. Uchendu ground his teeth audibly. Then he burst out:

'Never kill a man who says nothing. Those men of Abame were fools. What did they know about the man?' He ground his teeth again and told a story to illustrate his point. 'Mother Kite once sent her daughter to bring food. She went, and brought back a duckling. "You

98

have done very well," said Mother Kite to her daughter, "but tell me, what did the mother of this duckling say when you swooped and carried its child away?" "It said nothing," replied the young kite. "It just walked away." "You must return the duckling," said the Mother Kite. "There is something ominous behind the silence." And so Daughter Kite returned the duckling and took a chick instead.'"What did the mother of this chick do?" asked the old kite. "It cried and raved and cursed me," said the young kite. "Then we can eat the chick," said her mother. "There is nothing to fear from someone who shouts." Those men of Abame were fools.

'They were fools,' said Okonkwo after a pause. 'They had been warned that danger was ahead. They should have armed themselves with their guns and their matchets even when they went to market.'

'They have paid for their foolishness,' said Obierika. 'But I am greatly afraid. We have heard stories about white men who made the powerful guns and the strong drinks and took slaves away across the seas, but no one thought the stories were true.'

'There is no story that is not true,' said Uchendu. 'The world has no end, and what is good among one people is an abomination with others. We have albinos among us. Do you not think that they came to our clan by mistake, that they have strayed from their ways to a land where everybody is like them?'

◆

Okonkwo's first wife soon finished her cooking and set before their guests a big meal of pounded yams and bitter-leaf soup. Okonkwo's son, Nwoye, brought in a pot of sweet wine tapped from the raffia palm.

'You are a big man now,' Obierika said to Nwoye. 'Your friend Anene asked me to greet you.'

'Is he well?' asked Nwoye.

'We are all well,' said Obierika.

Ezinma brought them a bowl of water with which to wash their hands. After that they began to eat and to drink the wine.

'When did you set out from home?' asked Okonkwo.

'We had meant to set out from my house before cock-crow,' said

Obierika. 'But Nweke did not appear until it was quite light. Never make an early morning appointment with a man who has just married a new wife.' They all laughed.

'Has Nweke married a wife?' asked Okonkwo.

'He has married Okadigbo's second daughter,' said Obierika.

'That is very good,' said Okonkwo. 'I do not blame you for not hearing the cock crow.'

When they had eaten, Obierika pointed at the two heavy bags.

'That is the money from your yams,' he said. 'I sold the big ones as soon as you left. Later on I sold some of the seed-yams and gave out others to share-croppers. I shall do that every year until you return. But I thought you would need the money now and so I brought it. Who knows what may happen tomorrow? Perhaps green men will come to our clan and shoot us.'

'God will not permit it,' said Okonkwo. 'I do not know how to thank you.'

'I can tell you,' said Obierika. 'Kill one of your sons for me.'

'That will not be enough,' said Okonkwo.

'Then kill yourself,' said Obierika.

'Forgive me,' said Okonkwo, smiling. 'I shall not talk about thanking you any more.'

Chapter Sixteen

When nearly two years later Obierika paid another visit to his friend in exile the circumstances were less happy. The missionaries had come to Umuofia. They had built their church there, won a handful of converts and were already sending evangelists to the surrounding towns and villages. That was a source of great sorrow to the leaders of the clan; but many of them believed that the strange faith and the white man's god would not last. None of his converts was a man whose word was heeded in the assembly of the people. None of them was a man of title. They were mostly the kind of people that were called *efulefu*, worthless, empty men. The imagery of an *efulefu* in the language of the clan was a man who sold his matchet and wore the sheath to battle. Chielo, the priestess of Agbala, called the converts the excrement of the clan, and the new faith was a mad dog that had come to eat it up.

What moved Obierika to visit Okonkwo was the sudden appearance of the latter's son, Nwoye, among the missionaries in Umuofia.

'What are you doing here?' Obierika had asked when after many difficulties the missionaries had allowed him to speak to the boy.

'I am one of them,' replied Nwoye.

'How is your father?' Obierika asked, not knowing what else to say.

'I don't know. He is not my father,' said Nwoye, unhappily.

And so Obierika went to Mbanta to see his friend. And he found that Okonkwo did not wish to speak about Nwoye. It was only from Nwoye's mother that he heard scraps of the story.

◆

The arrival of the missionaries had caused a considerable stir in the village of Mbanta. There were six of them and one was a white man. Every man and woman came out to see the white man. Stories about these strange men had grown since one of them had been killed in Abame and his iron horse tied to the sacred silk-cotton tree. And so everybody came to see the white man. It was the time of the year when everybody was at home. The harvest was over.

When they had all gathered, the white man began to speak to them. He spoke through an interpreter who was an Ibo man, though his dialect was different and harsh to the ears of Mbanta. Many people laughed at his dialect and the way he used words strangely. Instead of saying "myself" he always said "my buttocks". But he was a man of commanding presence and the clansmen listened to him. He said he was one of them, as they could see from his colour and his language. The other four black men were also their brothers, although one of them did not speak Ibo. The white man was also their brother because they were all sons of God. And he told them about this new God, the Creator of all the world and all the men and women. He told them that they worshipped false gods, gods of wood and stone. A deep murmur went through the crowd when he said this. He told them that the true God lived on high and that all men when they died went before Him for judgment. Evil men and all the heathen who in their blindness bowed to wood and stone were thrown into a fire that burned like palm-oil. But good men who worshipped the true God lived for ever in His happy kingdom. 'We have been sent by this great God to ask you to leave your wicked ways and false gods and turn to Him so that you may be saved when you die,' he said.

'Your buttocks understand our language,' said someone light-heartedly and the crowd laughed.

'What did he say?' the white man asked his interpreter. But before he could answer, another man asked a question: 'Where is the white man's horse?' he asked. The Ibo evangelists consulted among themselves and decided that the man probably meant bicycle. They told the white man and he smiled benevolently.

'Tell them,' he said, 'that I shall bring many iron horses when we have settled down among them. Some of them will even ride the iron horse themselves.' This was interpreted to them but very few of them heard. They were talking excitedly among themselves because the white man had said he was going to live among them. They had not thought about that.

At this point an old man said he had a question. 'Which is this god of yours,' he asked, 'the goddess of the earth, the god of the sky, Amadiora of the thunderbolt, or what?'

The interpreter spoke to the white man and he immediately gave his answer. 'All the gods you have named are not gods at all. They are gods of deceit who will tell you to kill your fellows and destroy innocent children. There is only one true God and He has made the earth, the sky, you and me and all of us.'

'If we leave our gods and follow your god,' asked another man, 'who will protect us from the anger of our neglected gods and ancestors?'

'Your gods are not alive and cannot do you any harm,' replied the white man. 'They are pieces of wood and stone.'

When this was interpreted to the men of Mbanta they broke into derisive laughter. These men must be mad, they said to themselves. How else could they say that Ani and Amadior were harmless? And Idemili and Ogwugwu too? And some of them began to go away.

Then the missionaries burst into song. It was one of those gay and rollicking tunes of evangelism which had the power of plucking at silent and dusty chords in the heart of an Ibo man. The interpreter explained each verse to the audience, some of whom now stood enthralled. It was a story of brothers who lived in darkness and in fear, ignorant of the love of God. It told of one sheep out on the hills, away from the gates of God and from the tender shepherd's care.

After the singing the interpreter spoke about the Son of God whose name was Jesu Kristi. Okonkwo, who only stayed in the hope that it might come to chasing the men out of the village or whipping them, now said:

'You told us with your own mouth that there was only one god. Now you talk about his son. He must have a wife, then.' The crowd agreed.

'I did not say He had a wife,' said the interpreter, somewhat lamely.

'Your buttocks said he had a son,' said the joker. 'So he must have a wife and all of them must have buttocks.'

The missionary ignored him and went on to talk about the Holy Trinity. At the end of it Okonkwo was fully convinced that the man was mad. Hs shrugged his shoulders and went away to tap his afternoon palm-wine.

But there was a young lad who had been captivated. His name was Nwoye, Okonkwo's first son. It was not the mad logic of the Trinity that captivated him. He did not understand it. It was the poetry of the new religion, something felt in the marrow. The hymn about brothers who sat in darkness and in fear seemed to answer a vague and persistent question that haunted his young soul – the question of the twins crying in the bush and the question of Ikemefuna who was killed. He felt a relief within as the hymn poured into his parched soul. The words of the hymn were like the drops of frozen rain melting on the dry plate of the panting earth. Nwoye's callow mind was greatly puzzled.

Chapter Seventeen

The missionaries spent their first four or five nights in the market-place, and went into the village in the morning to preach the gospel. They asked who the king of the village was, but the villagers told them that there was no king. 'We have men of high title and the chief priests and the elders,' they said.

It was not very easy getting the men of high title and the elders together after the excitement of the first day. But the missionaries persevered, and in the end they were received by the rulers of Mbanta. They asked for a plot of land to build their church.

Every clan and village had its 'evil forest'. In it were buried all those who died of the really evil diseases, like leprosy and smallpox. It was also the dumping ground for the potent fetishes of great medicine-men when they died. An 'evil forest' was, therefore, alive with sinister forces and powers of darkness. It was such a forest that the rulers of Mbanta gave to the missionaries. They did not really want them in their clan, and so they made them that offer which nobody in his right senses would accept.

'They want a piece of land to build their shrine,' said Uchendu to his peers when they consulted among themselves. 'We shall give them a piece of land.' He paused, and there was a murmur of surprise and disagreement. 'Let us give them a portion of the Evil Forest. They boast about victory over death. Let us give them a real battlefield in which to show their victory.' They laughed and agreed, and sent for the missionaries, whom they had asked to leave them for a while so that they might 'whisper together'. They offered them as much of the Evil Forest as they cared to take. And to their greatest amazement the missionaries thanked them and burst into song.

'They do not understand,' said some of the elders. 'But they will understand when they go to their plot of land tomorrow morning.' And they dispersed.

The next morning the crazy men actually began to clear a part of the forest and to build their house. The inhabitants of Mbanta expected them all to be dead within four days. The first day passed and the second and third and fourth, and none of them died. Everyone was puzzled. And then it became known that the white man's fetish had unbelievable power. It was said that he wore glasses on his eyes so that he could see and talk to evil spirits. Not long after, he won his first three converts.

♦

Although Nwoye had been attracted to the new faith from the very first day, he kept it secret. He dared not go too near the missionaries for fear of his father. But whenever they came to preach in the open market-place or the village playground, Nwoye was there. And he was already beginning to know some of the simple stories they told.

'We have now built a church,' said Mr Kiaga, the interpreter, who was now in charge of the infant congregation. The white man had gone back to Umuofia, where he built his headquarters and from where he paid regular visits to Mr Kiaga's congregation at Mbanta.

'We have now built a church,' said Mr Kiaga, 'and we want you all to come in every seventh day to worship the true God.'

On the following Sunday, Nwoye passed and re-passed the little red-earth and thatch building without summoning enough courage to enter. He heard the voice of singing and although it came from a handful of men it was loud and confident. Their church stood on a circular clearing that looked like the open mouth of the Evil Forest. Was it waiting to snap its teeth together? After passing and re-passing by the church, Nwoye returned home.

It was well known among the people of Mbanta that their gods and ancestors were sometimes long-suffering and would deliberately allow a man to go on defying them. But even in such cases they set their limit at seven market weeks or twenty-eight days. Beyond that limit no man was suffered to go. And so excitement mounted in the village as the seventh week approached since the impudent missionaries built

106

their church in the Evil Forest. The villagers were so certain about the doom that awaited these men that one or two converts thought it wise to suspend their allegiance to the new faith.

At last the day came by which all the missionaries should have died. But they were still alive, building a new red-earth and thatch house for their teacher, Mr Kiaga. That week they won a handful more converts. And for the first time they had a woman. Her name was Nneka, the wife of Amadi, who was a prosperous farmer. She was very heavy with child.

Nneka had had four previous pregnancies and childbirths. But each time she had borne twins, and they had been immediately thrown away. Her husband and his family were already becoming highly critical of such a woman and were not unduly perturbed when they found she had fled to join the Christians. It was a good riddance.

◆

One morning Okonkwo's cousin, Amikwu, was passing by the church on his way from the neighbouring village, when he saw Nwoye among the Christians. He was greatly surprised, and when he got home he went straight to Okonkwo's hut and told him what he had seen. The women began to talk excitedly, but Okonkwo sat unmoved.

It was late afternoon before Nwoye returned. He went into the *obi* and saluted his father, but he did not answer. Nwoye turned round to walk into the inner compound when his father, suddenly overcome with fury, sprang to his feet and gripped him by the neck.

'Where have you been?' he stammered

Nwoye struggled to free himself from the choking grip.

'Answer me,' roared Okonkwo, 'before I kill you!' He seized a heavy stick that lay on the dwarf wall and hit him two or three savage blows.

'Answer me!' he roared again. Nwoye stood looking at him and did not say a word. The women were screaming outside, afraid to go in.

'Leave that boy at once!' said a voice in the outer compound. It was Okonkwo's uncle Uchendu. 'Are you mad?'

Okonkwo did not answer. But he left hold of Nwoye, who walked away and never returned.

He went back to the church and told Mr Kiaga that he had decided to go to Umuofia, where the white missionary had set up a school to teach young Christians to read and write.

Mr Kiaga's joy was very great. 'Blessed is he who forsakes his father and his mother for my sake,' he intoned. 'Those that hear my words are my father and my mother.'

Nwoye did not fully understand. But he was happy to leave his father. He would return later to his mother and his brothers and sisters and convert them to the new faith.

As Okonkwo sat in his hut that night, gazing into a log fire, he thought over the matter. A sudden fury rose within him and he felt a strong desire to take up his matchet, go to the church and wipe out the entire vile and miscreant gang. But on further thought he told himself that Nwoye was not worth fighting for. Why, he cried in his heart, should he, Okonkwo, of all people be cursed with such a son? He saw clearly in it the finger of his personal god or *chi*. For how else could he explain his great misfortune and exile and now his despicable son's behaviour? Now that he had time to think of it, his son's crime stood out in stark enormity. To abandon the gods of one's father and go about with a lot of effeminate men clucking like old hens was the very depth of abomination. Suppose when he died all his male children decided to follow Nwoye's steps and abandon their ancestors? Okonkwo felt a cold shudder run through him at the terrible prospect, like the prospect of annihilation. He saw himself and his father crowding round their ancestral shrine waiting in vain for worship and sacrifice and finding nothing but ashes of bygone days, and his children the while praying to the white man's god. If such a thing were ever to happen, he, Okonkwo, would wipe them off the face of the earth.

Okonkwo was popularly called the 'Roaring Flame'. As he looked into the log fire he recalled the name. He was a flaming fire. How then could he have begotten a son like Nwoye, degenerate and effeminate? Perhaps he was not his son. No! he could not be. His wife had played him false. He would teach her! But Nwoye resembled his grandfather, Unoka, who was Okonkwo's father. He pushed the thought out of his mind. He, Okonkwo, was called a flaming fire. How could he have begotten a woman for a son? At Nwoye's age Okonkwo had already become famous throughout Umuofia for his wrestling and his fearlessness.

He sighed heavily, and as if in sympathy the smouldering log also sighed. And immediately Okonkwo's eyes were opened and he saw the whole matter clearly. Living fire begets cold, impotent ash. He sighed again, deeply.

Chapter Eighteen

The young church in Mbanta had a few crises early in its life. At first the clan had assumed that it would not survive. But it had gone on living and gradually becoming stronger. The clan was worried, but not overmuch. If a gang of *efulefu* decided to live in the Evil Forest it was their own affair. When one came to think of it, the Evil Forest was a fit home for such undesirable people. It was true they were rescuing twins from the bush, but they never brought them into the village. As far as the villagers were concerned, the twins still remained where they had been thrown away. Surely the earth goddess would not visit the sins of the missionaries on the innocent villagers?

But on one occasion the missionaries had tried to overstep the bounds. Three converts had gone into the village and boasted openly that all the gods were dead and impotent and that they were prepared to defy them by burning all their shrines.

'Go and burn your mothers' genitals,' said one of the priests. The men were seized and beaten until they streamed with blood. After that nothing happened for a long time between the church and the clan.

But stories were already gaining ground that the white man had not only brought a religion but also a government. It was said that they had built a place of judgement in Umuofia to protect the followers of their religion. It was even said that they had hanged one man who killed a missionary.

Although such stories were now often told they looked like fairy-tales in Mbanta and did not as yet affect the relationship between the new church and the clan. There was no question of killing a missionary here, for Mr Kiaga, despite his madness, was quite harmless. As for his converts, no one could kill them without having to flee from the clan, for in spite of their worthlessness they still belonged to the clan.

And so nobody gave serious thought to the stories about the white man's government or the consequences of killing the Christians. If they became more troublesome than they already were they would simply be driven out of the clan.

And the little church was at that moment too deeply absorbed in its own troubles to annoy the clan. It all began over the question of admitting outcasts.

These outcasts, or *osu*, seeing that the new religion welcomed twins and such abominations, thought that it was possible that they would also be received. And so one Sunday two of them went into the church. There was an immediate stir; but so great was the work the new religion had done among the converts that they did not immediately leave the church when the outcasts came in. Those who found themselves nearest to them merely moved to another seat. It was a miracle. But it only lasted till the end of the service. The whole church raised a protest and were about to drive these people out, when Mr Kiaga stopped them and began to explain.

'Before God,' he said, 'there is no slave or free. We are all children of God and we must receive these our brothers.'

'You do not understand,' said one of the converts. 'What will the heathen say of us when they hear that we receive *osu* into our midst? They will laugh.'

'Let them laugh,' said Mr Kiaga. 'God will laugh at them on the judgment day. Why do the nations rage and the peoples imagine a vain thing? He that sitteth in the heavens shall laugh. The Lord shall have them in derision.'

'You do not understand,' the convert maintained. 'You are our teacher, and you can teach us the things of the new faith. But this is a matter which we know.' And he told him what an *osu* was.

He was a person dedicated to a god, a thing set apart – a taboo for ever, and his children after him. He could neither marry nor be married by the free-born. He was in fact an outcast, living in a special area of the village, close to the Great Shrine. Wherever he went he carried with him the mark of his forbidden caste – long, tangled and dirty hair. A razor was taboo to him. An *osu* could not attend an assembly of the free-born, and they, in turn, could not shelter under his roof. He could not take any of the four titles of the clan, and when

111

he died he was buried by his kind in the Evil Forest. How could such a man be a follower of Christ?

'He needs Christ more than you and I,' said Mr Kiaga.

'Then I shall go back to the clan,' said the convert. And he went. Mr Kiaga stood firm, and it was his firmness that saved the young church. The wavering converts drew inspiration and confidence from his unshakable faith. He ordered the outcasts to shave off their long, tangled hair. At first they were afraid they might die.

'Unless you shave off the mark of your heathen belief I will not admit you into the church,' said Mr Kiaga. 'You fear that you will die. Why should that be? How are you different from other men who shave their hair? The same God created you and them. But they have cast you out like lepers. It is against the will of God, who has promised everlasting life to all who believe in His holy name. The heathen say you will die if you do this or that, and you are afraid. They also said I would die if I built my church on this ground. Am I dead? They said I would die if I took care of twins. I am still alive. The heathen speak nothing but falsehood. Only the word of our God is true.'

The two outcasts shaved off their hair, and soon they were among the strongest adherents of the new faith. And what was more, nearly all the *osu* in Mbanta followed their example. It was in fact one of them who in his zeal brought the church into serious conflict with the clan a year later by killing the sacred python, the emanation of the god of water.

The royal python was the most revered animal in Mbanta and all the surrounding clans. It was addressed as 'Our Father', and was allowed to go wherever it chose, even into people's beds. It ate rats in the house and sometimes swallowed hens' eggs. If a clansman killed a royal python accidentally, he made sacrifices of atonement and performed an expensive burial ceremony such as was done for a great man. No punishment was prescribed for a man who killed the python knowingly. Nobody thought that such a thing could ever happen.

Perhaps it never did happen. That was the way the clan at first looked at it. No one had actually seen the man do it. The story had arisen among the Christians themselves.

But, all the same, the rulers and elders of Mbanta assembled to decide on their action. Many of them spoke at great length and in fury. The spirit of war was upon them. Okonkwo, who had begun to play a part in the affairs of his motherland, said that until the abominable gang was chased out of the village with whips there would be no peace.

But there were many others who saw the situation differently, and it was their counsel that prevailed in the end.

'It is not our custom to fight for our gods,' said one of them. 'Let us not presume to do so now. If a man kills the sacred python in the secrecy of his hut, the matter lies between him and the god. We did not see it. If we put ourselves between the god and his victim we may receive blows intended for the offender. When a man blasphemes what do we do? Do we go and stop his mouth? No. We put our fingers into our ears to stop us hearing. That is a wise action.'

'Let us not reason like cowards,' said Okonkwo. 'If a man comes into my hut and defaecates on the floor, what do I do? Do I shut my eyes? No! I take a stick and break his head. That is what a man does. These people are daily pouring filth over us, and Okeke says we should pretend not to see.' Okonkwo made a sound full of disgust. This was a womanly clan, he thought. Such a thing could never happen in his fatherland, Umuofia.

'Okonkwo has spoken the truth,' said another man. 'We should do something. But let us ostracise these men. We would then not be held accountable for their abominations.'

Everybody in the assembly spoke, and in the end it was decided to ostracise the Christians. Okonkwo ground his teeth in disgust.

◆

That night a bell-man went through the length and breadth of Mbanta proclaiming that the adherents of the new faith were thenceforth excluded from the life and privileges of the clan.

The Christians had grown in number and were now a small community of men, women and children, self-assured and confident. Mr Brown, the white missionary, paid regular visits to them. 'When I think that it is only eighteen months since the Seed was first sown among you,' he said, 'I marvel at what the Lord hath wrought.'

It was Wednesday in Holy week and Mr Kiaga had asked the

women to bring red earth and white chalk and water to scrub the church for Easter, and the women had formed themselves into three groups for this purpose. They set out early that morning, some of them with their water-pots to the stream, another group with hoes and baskets to the village red-earth pit, and the others to the chalk quarry.

Mr Kiaga was praying in the church when he heard the women talking excitedly. He rounded off his prayer and went to see what it was all about. The women had come to the church with empty water-pots. They said that some young men had chased them away from the stream with whips. Soon after, the women who had gone for red earth returned with empty baskets. Some of them had been heavily whipped. The chalk women also returned to tell a similar story.

'What does it all mean?' asked Mr Kiaga, who was greatly perplexed.

'The village has outlawed us,' said one of the women. 'The bell-man announced it last night. But it is not our custom to debar anyone from the stream or the quarry.'

Another woman said, 'They want to ruin us. They will not allow us into the markets. They have said so.'

Mr Kiaga was going to send into the village for his men-converts when he saw them coming on their own. Of course they had all heard the bell-man, but they had never in all their lives heard of women being debarred from the stream.

'Come along,' they said to the women. 'We will go with you to meet those cowards.' Some of them had big sticks and some even matchets.

But Mr Kiaga restrained them. He wanted first to know why they had been outlawed.

'They say that Okoli killed the sacred python,' said one man.

'It is false,' said another. 'Okoli told me himself that it was false.'

Okoli was not there to answer. He had fallen ill on the previous night. Before the day was over he was dead. His death showed that the gods were still able to fight their own battles. The clan saw no reason then for molesting the Christians.

Chapter Nineteen

The last big rains of the year were falling. It was the time for treading red earth with which to build walls. It was not done earlier because the rains were too heavy and would have washed away the heap of trodden earth; and it could not be done later because harvesting would soon set in, and after that the dry season.

It was going to be Okonkwo's last harvest in Mbanta. The seven wasted and weary years were at last dragging to a close. Although he had prospered in his motherland Okonkwo knew that he would have prospered even more in Umuofia, in the land of his fathers where men were bold and warlike. In these seven years he would have climbed to the utmost heights. And so he regretted every day of his exile. His mother's kinsmen had been very kind to him, and he was grateful. But that did not alter the facts. He had called the first child born to him in exile Nneka – 'Mother is Supreme' – out of politeness to his mother's kinsmen. But two years later when a son was born he called him Nwofia – 'Begotten in the Wilderness'.

As soon as he entered his last year in exile Okonkwo sent money to Obierika to build him two huts in his old compound where he and his family would live until he built more huts and the outside wall of his compound. He could not ask another man to build his own *obi* for him, nor the walls of his compound. Those things a man built for himself or inherited from his father.

As the last heavy rains of the year began to fall, Obierika sent word that the two huts had been built and Okonkwo began to prepare for his return, after the rains. He would have liked to return earlier and build his compound that year before the rains stopped, but in doing so he would have taken something from the full penalty of seven years. And that could not be. So he waited impatiently for the dry season to come.

It came slowly. The rain became lighter and lighter until it fell in slanting showers. Sometimes the sun shone through the rain and a light breeze blew. It was a gay and airy kind of rain. The rainbow began to appear, and sometimes two rainbows, like a mother and her daughter, the one young and beautiful, and the other an old and faint shadow. The rainbow was called the python of the sky.

Okonkwo called his three wives and told them to get things together for a great feast. 'I must thank my mother's kinsmen before I go,' he said.

Ekwefi still had some cassava left on her farm from the previous year. Neither of the other wives had. It was not that they had been lazy, but that they had many children to feed. It was therefore understood that Ekwefi would provide cassava for the feast. Nwoye's mother and Ojiugo would provide the other things like smoked fish, palm-oil and pepper for the soup. Okonkwo would take care of meat and yams.

Ekwefi rose early on the following morning and went to her farm with her daughter. Ezinma, and Ojiugo's daughter, Obiageli, to harvest cassava tubers. Each of them carried a long cane basket, a matchet for cutting down the soft cassava stem, and a little hoe for digging out the tuber. Fortunately, a light rain had fallen during the night and the soil would not be very hard.

'It will not take us long to harvest as much as we like,' said Ekwefi.

'But the leaves will be wet,' said Ezinma. Her basket was balanced on her head, and her arms folded across her breasts. She felt cold. 'I dislike cold water dropping on my back. We should have waited for the sun to rise and dry the leaves.'

Obiageli called her 'Salt' because she said that she disliked water. 'Are you afraid you may dissolve?'

The harvesting was easy, as Ekwefi had said. Ezinma shook every tree violently with a long stick before she bent down to cut the stem and dig out the tuber. Sometimes it was not necessary to dig. They just pulled the stump and earth rose, roots snapped below, and the tuber was pulled out.

When they had harvested a sizeable heap they carried it down in two trips to the steam, where every woman had a shallow well for fermenting her cassava.

116

'It should be ready in four days or even three,' said Obiagli. 'They are young tubers.'

'They are not all that young,' said Ekwefi. 'I planted the farm nearly two years ago. It is a poor soil and that is why the tubers are so small.'

◆

Okonkwo never did things by halves. When his wife Ekwefi protested that two goats were sufficient for the feast he told her that it was not her affair.

'I am calling a feast because I have the wherewithal. I cannot live on the bank of a river and wash my hands with spittle. My mother's people have been good to me and I must show my gratitude.'

And so three goats were slaughtered and a number of fowls. It was like a wedding feast. There was foo-foo and yam pottage, egusi soup and bitter-leaf soup and pots and pots of palm-wine.

All the *umunna* were invited to the feast, all the descendants of Okolo, who had lived about two hundred years before. The oldest member of this extensive family was Okonkwo's uncle, Uchendu. The kola nut was given to him to break, and he prayed to the ancestors. He asked them for health and children. 'We do not ask for wealth because he that has health and children will also have wealth. We do not pray to have more money but to have more kinsmen. We are better than animals because we have kinsmen. An animal rubs its aching flank against a tree, a man asks his kinsman to scratch him.' He prayed especially for Okonkwo and his family. He then broke the kola nut and threw one of the lobes on the ground for the ancestors.

As the broken kola nuts were passed round, Okonkwo's wives and children and those who came to help them with the cooking began to bring out the food. His sons brought out the pots of palm-wine. There was so much food and drink that many kinsmen whistled in surprise. When all was laid out, Okonkwo rose to speak.

'I beg you to accept this little kola,' he said. 'It is not to pay you back for all you did for me in these seven years. A child cannot pay for its mother's milk. I have only called you together because it is good for kinsmen to meet.'

Yam pottage was served first because it was lighter than foo-foo

117

and because yam always came first. Then the foo-foo was served. Some kinsmen ate it with egusi soup and others with bitter-leaf soup. The meat was then shared so that every member of the *umunna* had a portion. Every man rose in order of years and took a share. Even the few kinsmen who had not been able to come had their shares taken out for them in due turn.

As the palm-wine was drunk one of the oldest members of the *umunna* rose to thank Okonkwo:

'If I say that we did not expect such a big feast I will be suggesting that we did not know how open-handed our son, Okonkwo is. We all know him, and we expected a big feast. But it turned out to be even bigger than we expected. Thank you. May all you took out return again tenfold. It is good in these days when the younger generation consider themselves wiser than their sires to see a man doing things in the grand, old way. A man who calls his kinsmen to a feast does not do so to save them from starving. They all have food in their own homes. When we gather together in the moonlit village ground it is not because of the moon. Every man can see it in his own compound. We come together because it is good for kinsmen to do so. You may ask why I am saying all this. I say it because I fear for the younger generation, for you people.' He waved his arm where most of the young men sat, 'As for me, I have only a short while to live, and so have Uchendu and Unachukwu and Emefo. But I fear for you young people because you do not understand how strong is the bond of kinship. You do not know what it is to speak with one voice. And what is the result? An abominable religion has settled among you. A man can now leave his father and his brothers. He can curse the gods of his fathers and his ancestors, like a hunter's dog that suddenly goes mad and turns on his master. I fear for you; I fear for the clan.' He turned again to Okonkwo and said, 'Thank you for calling us together.'

PART THREE

Chapter Twenty

Seven years was a long time to be away from one's clan. A man's place was not always there, waiting for him. As soon as he left, someone else rose and filled it. The clan was like a lizard; if it lost its tail it soon grew another.

Olonkwo knew these things. He knew that he had lost his place among the nine masked spirits who administered justice in the clan. He had lost the chance to lead his warlike clan against the new religion, which, he was told, had gained ground. He had lost the years in which he might have taken the highest titles in the clan. But some of these losses were not irreparable. He was determined that his return should be marked by his people. He would return with a flourish, and regain the seven wasted years.

Even in his first year in exile he had begun to plan for his return. The first thing he would do would be to rebuild his compound on a more magnificent scale. He would build a bigger barn than he had before and he would build huts for two new wives. Then he would show his wealth by initiating his sons in the *ozo* society. Only the really great men in the clan were able to do this. Okonkwo saw clearly the high esteem in which he would be held, and he saw himself taking the highest title in the land.

As the years of exile passed one by one it seemed to him that his *chi* might now be making amends for the past disaster. His yams grew abundantly, not only in his motherland but also in Umuofia, where his friend gave them out year by year to share-croppers.

Then the tragedy of his first son had occurred. At first it appeared as if it might prove too great for his spirit. But it was a resilient spirit, and in the end Okonkwo overcame his sorrow. He had five other sons and he would bring them up in the way of the clan.

121

He sent for the five sons and they came and sat in his *obi*. The youngest of them was four years old.

'You have all seen the great abomination of your brother. Now he is no longer my son or your brother. I will only have a son who is a man, who will hold his head up among my people. If any one of you prefers to be a woman, let him follow Nwoye now while I am alive so that I can curse him. If you turn against me when I am dead I will visit you and break your neck.'

Okonkwo was very lucky in his daughters. He never stopped regretting that Ezinma was a girl. Of all his children she alone understood his every mood. A bond of sympathy had grown between them as the years had passed.

Ezinma grew up in her father's exile and became one of the most beautiful girls in Mbanta. She was called Crystal of Beauty, as her mother had been called in her youth. The young ailing girl who had caused her mother so much heartache had been tranformed, almost overnight, into a healthy, buoyant maiden. She had, it was true, her moments of depression when she would snap at everybody like an angry dog. These moods descended on her suddenly and for no apparent reason. But they were very rare and short-lived. As long as they lasted, she could bear no other person but her father.

Many young men and prosperous middle-aged men of Mbanta came to marry her. But she refused them all, because her father had called her one evening and said to her: 'There are many good and prosperous people here, but I shall be happy if you marry in Umuofia when we return home.'

That was all he had said. But Ezinma had seen clearly all the thought and hidden meaning behind the few words. And she had agreed.

'Your half-sister, Obiageli, will not understand me,' Okonkwo said. 'But you can explain to her.'

Although they were almost the same age. Ezinma wielded a strong influence over her half-sister. She explained to her why they should not marry yet, and she agreed also. And so the two of them refused every offer of marraige in Mbanta.

'I wish she were a boy,' Okonkwo thought within himself. She understood things so perfectly. Who else among his children could have read his thought so well? With two beautiful grown-up daughters his return to Umuofia would attract considerable attention. His future sons-in-law would be men of authority in the clan. The poor and unknown would not dare to come forth.

Umuofia had indeed changed during the seven years Okonkwo had been in exile. The church had come and led many astray. Not only the low-born and the outcast but sometimes a worthy man had joined it. Such a man was Ogbuefi Ugonna, who had taken two titles, and who like a madman had cut the anklet of his titles and cast it away to join the Christians. The white missionary was very proud of him and he was one of the first men in Umuofia to receive the sacrament of Holy Communion, or Holy Feast as it was called in Ibo. Ogbuefi Ugonna had thought of the Feast in terms of eating and drinking, only more holy than the village variety. He had therefore put his drinking-horn into his goatskin bag for the occasion.

But apart from the church, the white men had also brought a government. They had built a court where the District Commissioner judged cases in ignorance. He had court messengers who brought men to him for trial. Many of these messengers came from Umuru on the bank of the Great River, where the white men first came many years before and where they had built the centre of their religion and trade and government. These court messengers were greatly hated in Umuofia because they were foreigners and also arrogant and high-handed. They were called *kotma*, and because of their ash-coloured shorts they earned the additional name of Ashy-Buttocks. They guarded the prison, which was full of men who had offended against the white man's law. Some of these prisoners had thrown away their twins and some had molested the Christians. They were beaten in the prison by the *kotma* and made to work every morning clearing the government compound and fetching wood for the white Commissioner and the court messengers. Some of these prisoners were men of title who should be above such mean occupation. They were grieved by the indignity and mourned for their neglected farms. As they cut grass in the morning the younger men sang in time with the strokes of their matchets:

> 'Kotma *of the ash buttocks,*
> *He is fit to be a slave*

The white man has no sense,
He is fit to be a slave'

The court messengers did not like to be called Ashy-Buttocks, and they beat the men. But the song spread in Umuofia.

Okonkwo's head was bowed in sadness as Obierika told him these things.

'Perhaps I have been away too long,' Okonkwo said, almost to himself. 'But I cannot understand these things you tell me. What is it that has happened to our people? Why have they lost the power to fight?'

'Have you not heard how the white man wiped out Abame?' asked Obierika.

'I have heard,' said Okonkwo. 'But I have also heard that Abame people were weak and foolish. Why did they not fight back? Had they no guns and matchets? We would be cowards to compare ourselves with the men of Abame. Their fathers had never dared to stand before our ancestors. We must fight these men and drive them from the land.'

'It is already too late,' said Obierika sadly. 'Our own men and our sons have joined the ranks of the stranger. They have joined his religion and they help to uphold his government. If we should try to drive out the white men in Umuofia we should find it easy. There are only two of them. But what of our own people who are following their way and have been given power? They would go to Umuru and bring the soldiers, and we would be like Abame.' He paused for a long time and then said: 'I told you on my last visit to Mbanta how they hanged Aneto.'

'What has happened to that piece of land in dispute?' asked Okonkwo.

'The white man's court has decided that it should belong to Nnama's family, who had given much money to the white man's messengers and interpreter.'

'Does the white man understand our custom about land?'

'How can he when he does not even speak our tongue? But he says that our customs are bad; and our own brothers who have taken up his religion also say that our customs are bad. How do you think we can fight when our own brothers have turned against us? The white man is very clever. He came quietly and peaceably with his religion. We were amused at his foolishness and allowed him to stay. Now he has won our brothers, and our clan can no longer act like one. He has put a knife on the things that held us together and we have fallen apart.'

'How did they get hold of Aneto to hang him?' asked Okonkwo.

'When he killed Oduche in the fight over the land, he fled to Aninta to escape the wrath of the earth. This was about eight days after the fight, because Oduche had not died immediately from his wounds. It was on the seventh day that he died. But everybody knew that he was going to die and Aneto got his belongings together in readiness to flee. But the Christians had told the white man about the accident, and he sent his *kotma* to catch Aneto. He was imprisoned with all the leaders of his family. In the end Oduche died and Aneto was taken to Umuru and hanged. The other people were released, but even now they have not found the mouth with which to tell of their suffering.'

The two men sat in silence for a long while afterwards.

Chapter Twenty-One

There were many men and women in Umuofia who did not feel as strongly as Okonkwo about the new dispensation. The white man had indeed brought a lunatic religion, but he had also built a trading store and for the first time palm-oil and kernel became things of great price, and much money flowed into Umuofia.

And even in the matter of religion there was a growing feeling that there might be something in it after all, something vaguely akin to method in the overwhelming madness.

This growing feeling was due to Mr Brown, the white missionary, who was very firm in restraining his flock from provoking the wrath of the clan. One member in particular was very difficult to restrain. His name was Enoch and his father was the priest of the snake cult. The story went around that Enoch had killed and eaten the sacred python, and that his father had cursed him.

Mr Brown preached against such excess of zeal. Every thing was possible, he told his energetic flock, but everything was not expedient. And so Mr Brown came to be respected even by the clan, because he trod softly on its faith. He made friends with some of the great men of the clan and on one of his frequent visits to the neighbouring villages he had been presented with a carved elephant tusk, which was a sign of dignity and rank. One of the great men in that village was called Akunna and he had given one of his sons to be taught the white man's knowledge in Mr Brown's school.

Whenever Mr Brown went to that village he spent long hours with Akunna in his *obi* talking through an interpreter about religion. Neither of them succeeded in converting the other but they learnt more about their different beliefs.

'You say that there is one supreme God who made heaven and earth,' said Akunna on one of Mr Brown's visits. 'We also believe in

Him and call Him Chukwu. He made all the world and the other gods.'

'There are no other gods,' said Mr Brown. 'Chukwu is the only God and all others are false. You carve a piece of wood – like that one' (he pointed at the rafters from which Akunna's carved *Ikenga* hung), 'and you call it a god. But it is still a piece of wood.'

'Yes,' said Akunna. 'It is indeed a piece of wood. The tree from which it came was made by Chukwu, as indeed all minor gods were. But He made them for His messengers so that we could approach Him through them. It is like yourself. You are the head of your church.'

'No,' protested Mr Brown. 'The head of my church is God Himself.'

'I know,' said Akunna, 'but there must be a head in this world among men. Somebody like yourself must be the head here.'

'The head of my church in that sense is in England.'

'That is exactly what I am saying. The head of your church is in your country. He has sent you here as his messenger. And you have also appointed your own messengers and servants. Or let me take another example, the District Commissioner. He is sent by your king.'

'They have a queen,' said the interpreter on his own account.

'Your queen sends her messenger, the District Commissioner. He finds that he cannot do the work alone and so he appoints *kotma* to help him. It is the same with God, or Chukwu. He appoints the smaller gods to help Him because His work is too great for one person.'

'You should not think of him as a person,' said Mr Brown. 'It is because you do so that you imagine He must need helpers. And the worst thing about it is that you give all the worship to the false gods you have created.'

'That is not so. We make sacrifices to the little gods, but when they fail and there is no one else to turn to we go to Chukwu. It is right to do so. We approach a great man through his servants. But when his servants fail to help us, then we go to the last source of hope. We appear to pay greater attention to the little gods but that is not so. We worry them more because we are afraid to worry their Master. Our fathers knew that Chukwu was the Overlord and that is why many of them gave their children the name Chukwuka – "Chukwu is Supreme".'

'You said one interesting thing,' said Mr Brown. 'You are afraid of

Chukwu. In my religion Chukwu is a loving Father and need not be feared by those who do His will.'

'But we must fear Him when we are not doing His will,' said Akunna. 'And who is to tell His will? It is too great to be known.'

In this way Mr Brown learnt a good deal about the religion of the clan and he came to the conclusion that a frontal attack on it would not succeed. And so he built a school and a little hospital in Umuofia. He went from family to family begging people to send their children to his school. But at first they only sent their slaves or sometimes their lazy children. Mr Brown begged and argued and prophesied. He said that the leaders of the land in the future would be men and women who had learnt to read and write. If Umuofia failed to send her children to the school, strangers would come from other places to rule them. They could already see that happening in the Native Court, where the D.C. was surrounded by strangers who spoke his tongue. Most of these strangers came from the distant town of Umuru on the bank of the Great River where the white man first went.

In the end Mr Brown's arguments began to have an effect. More people came to learn in his school, and he encouraged them with gifts of singlets and towels. They were not all young, these people who came to learn. Some of them were thirty years old or more. They worked on their farms in the morning and went to school in the afternoon. And it was not long before the people began to say that the white man's medicine was quick in working. Mr Brown's school produced quick results. A few months in it were enough to make one a court messenger or even a court clerk. Those who stayed longer became teachers; and from Umuofia labourers went forth into the Lord's vineyard. New churches were established in the surrounding villages and a few schools with them. From the very beginning religion and education went hand in hand.

Mr Brown's mission grew from strength to strength, and because of its link with the new administration it earned a new social prestige. But Mr Brown himself was breaking down in health. At first he ignored the warning signs. But in the end he had to leave his flock, sad and broken.

◆

It was in the first rainy season after Okonkwo's return to Umuofia that Mr Brown left for home. As soon as he had learnt of Okonkwo's return five months earlier, the missionary had immediately paid him a visit. He had just sent Okonkwo's son, Nwoye, who was now called Isaac, to the new training college for teachers in Umuru. And he had hoped that Okonkwo would be happy to hear of it. But Okonkwo had driven him away with the threat that if he came into his compound again, he would be carried out of it.

Okonkwo's return to his native land was not as memorable as he had wished. It was true his two beautiful daughters aroused great interest among suitors and marriage negotiations were soon in progress, but, beyond that, Umuofia did not appear to have taken any special notice of the warrior's return. The clan had undergone such profound change during his exile that it was barely recognizable. The new religion and government and the trading stores were very much in the people's eyes and minds. There were still many who saw these new institutions as evil, but even they talked and thought about little else, and certainly not about Okonkwo's return.

And it was the wrong year too. If Okonkwo had immediately initiated his two sons into the *ozo* society as he had planned he would have caused a stir. But the initiation rite was performed once in three years in Umuofia, and he had to wait for nearly two years for the next round of ceremonies.

Okonkwo was deeply grieved. And it was not just a personal grief. He mourned for the clan, which he saw breaking up and falling apart, and he mourned for the warlike men of Umuofia, who had so unaccountably become soft like women.

Chapter Twenty-Two

Mr Brown's successor was the Reverend James Smith, and he was a different kind of man. He condemned openly Mr Brown's policy of compromise and accommodation. He saw things as black and white. And black was evil. He saw the world as a battlefield in which the children of light were locked in mortal conflict with the sons of darkness. He spoke in his sermons about sheep and goats and about wheat and tares. He believed in slaying the prophets of Baal.

Mr Smith was greatly distressed by the ignorance which many of his flock showed even in such things as the Trinity and the Sacraments. It only showed that they were seeds sown on a rocky soil. Mr Brown had thought of nothing but numbers., He should have known that the kingdom of God did not depend on large crowds. Our Lord Himself stressed the importance of fewness. Narrow is the way and few the number. To fill the Lord's holy temple with an idolatrous crowd clamouring for signs was a folly of everlasting consequence. Our Lord used the whip only once in His Life – to drive the crowd away from His church.

Within a few weeks of his arrival in Umuofia Mr Smith suspended a young woman from the church for pouring new wine into old bottles. This woman had allowed her heathen husband to mutilate her dead child. The child had been declared an *ogbanje*, plaguing its mother by dying and entering her womb to be born again. Four times this child had run its evil round. And so it was mutilated to discourage it from returning.

Mr Smith was filled with wrath when he heard of this. He disbelieved the story which even some of the most faithful confirmed, the story of really evil children who were not deterred by mutilation, but came back with all the scars. He replied that such stories were spread in the world by the Devil to lead men astray. Those who believed such stories were unworthy of the Lord's table.

There was a saying in Umuofia that as a man danced so the drums were beaten for him. Mr Smith danced a furious step and so the drums went mad. The over-zealous converts who had smarted under Mr Brown's restraining hand now flourished in full favour. One of them was Enoch, the son of the snake-priest who was believed to have killed and eaten the sacred python. Enoch's devotion to the new faith had seemed so much greater than Mr Brown's that the villagers called him The Outsider who wept louder than the bereaved.

Enoch was short and slight of build, and always seemed in great haste. His feet were short and broad, and when he stood or walked his heels came together and his feet opened outwards as if they had quarrelled and meant to go in different directions. Such was the excessive energy bottled up in Enoch's small body that it was always erupting in quarrels and fights. On Sundays he always imagined that the sermon was preached for the benefit of his enemies. And if he happened to sit near one of them he would occasionally turn to give him a meaningful look, as if to say, 'I told you so.' It was Enoch who touched off the great conflict between church and clan in Umuofia which had been gathering since Mr Brown left.

It happened during the annual ceremony which was held in honour of the earth deity. At such times the ancestors of the clan who had been committed to Mother Earth at their death emerged again as *egwugwu* through tiny ant-holes.

One of the greatest crimes a man could commit was to unmask an *egwugwu* in public, or to say or do anything which might reduce its immortal prestige in the eyes of the uninitiated. And this was what Enoch did.

The annual worship of the earth goddess fell on a Sunday, and the masked spirits were abroad. The Christian women who had been to church could not therefore go home. Some of their men had gone out to beg the *egwugwu* to retire for a short while for the women to pass. They agreed and were already retiring, when Enoch boasted aloud that they would not dare to touch a Christian. Whereupon they all came back and one of them gave Enoch a good stroke of the cane, which was always carried. Enoch fell on him and tore off his mask.

131

The other *egwugwu* immediately surrounded their desecrated companion, to shield him from the profane gaze of women and children, and led him away. Enoch had killed an ancestral spirit, and Umuofia was thrown into confusion.

That night the Mother of the Spirits walked the length and breadth of the clan, weeping for her murdered son. It was a terrible night. Not even the oldest man in Umuofia had ever heard such a strange and fearful sound, and it was never to be heard again. It seemed as if the very soul of the tribe wept for a great evil that was coming – its own death.

On the next day all the masked *egwugwu* of Umuofia assembled in the market-place. They came from all the quarters of the clan and even from the neighbouring villages. The dreadful Otakagu came from Imo, and Ekwensu, dangling a white cock, arrived from Uli. It was a terrible gathering. The eerie voices of countless spirits, the bells that clattered behind some of them, and the clash of matchets as they ran forwards and backwards and saluted one another, sent tremors of fear into every heart. For the first time in living memory the sacred bull-roarer was heard in broad daylight.

From the market-place the furious band made for Enoch's compound. Some of the elders of the clan went with them, wearing heavy protections of charms and amulets. These were men whose arms were strong in *ogwu*, or medicine. As for the ordinary men and women, they listened from the safety of their huts.

The leader of the Christians had met together at Mr Smith's parsonage on the previous night. As they deliberated they could hear the Mother of Spirits wailing for her son. The chilling sound affected Mr Smith, and for the first time he seemed to be afraid.

'What are they planning to do?' he asked. No one knew, because such a thing had never happened before. Mr Smith would have sent for the District Commissioner and his court messengers, but they had gone on tour on the previous day.

'One thing is clear,' said Mr Smith. 'We cannot offer physical resistance to them. Our strength lies in the Lord.' They knelt down together and prayed to God for delivery.

'O Lord save Thy people,' cried Mr Smith.

'And bless Thine inheritance,' replied the men.

They decided that Enoch should be hidden in the parsonage for a day or two. Enoch himself was greatly disappointed when he heard this, for he had hoped that a holy war was imminent; and there were a few other Christians who thought like him. But wisdom prevailed in the camp of the faithful and many lives were thus saved.

The band of *egwugwu* moved like a furious whirlwind to Enoch's compound and with matchet and fire reduced it to a desolate heap. And from there they made for the church, intoxicated with destruction.

Mr Smith was in his church when he heard the masked spirits coming. He walked quietly to the door which commanded the approach to the church compound, and stood there. But when the first three or four *egwugwu* appeared on the church compound he nearly bolted. He overcame this impulse and instead of running away he went down the two steps that led up to the church and walked towards the approaching spirits.

They surged forward, and a long stretch of the bamboo fence with which the church compound was surrounded gave way before them. Discordant bells clanged, matchets clashed and the air was full of dust and weird sounds. Mr Smith heard a sound of footsteps behind him. He turned round and saw Okeke, his interpreter. Okeke had not been on the best of terms with his master since he had strongly condemned Enoch's behaviour at the meeting of the leaders of the church during the night. Okeke had gone as far as to say that Enoch should not be hidden in the parsonage, because he would only draw the wrath of the clan on the pastor. Mr Smith had rebuked him in very strong language, and had not sought his advice that morning. But now, as he came up and stood by him confronting the angry spirits, Mr Smith looked at him and smiled. It was a wan smile, but there was deep gratitude there.

For a brief moment the onrush of the *egwugwu* was checked by the unexpected composure of the two men. But it was only a momentary check, like the tense silence between blasts of thunder. The second onrush was greater than the first. It swallowed up the two men. Then an unmistakable voice rose above the tumult and there was immediate silence. Space was made around the two men, and Ajofia began to speak.

Ajofia was the leading *egwugwu* of Umuofia. He was the head and spokeman of the nine ancestors who adminsitered justice in the clan. His voice was unmistakable and so he was able to bring immediate peace to the agitated spirits. He then addressed Mr Smith, and as he spoke clouds of smoke rose from his head.

'The body of the white man, I salute you,' he said, using the language in which immortals spoke to men.

'The body of the white man, do you know me?' he asked.

Mr Smith looked at his interpreter, but Okeke, who was a native of distant Umuru, was also at a loss.

Ajofia laughed in his gutteral voice. It was like the laugh of rusty metal. 'They are strangers,' he said, 'and they are ignorant. But let that pass.' He turned round to his comrades and saluted them, calling them the fathers of Umuofia. He dug his rattling spear into the ground and it shook with metallic life. Then he turned once more to the missionary and his interpreter.

'Tell the white man that we will not do him any harm,' he said to the interpreter. 'Tell him to go back to his house and leave us alone. We liked his brother who was with us before. He was foolish, but we liked him, and for his sake we shall not harm his brother. But this shrine which he built must be destroyed. We shall no longer allow it in our midst. It has bred untold abominations and we have come to put an end to it.' He turned to his comrades, 'Fathers of Umuofia, I salute you;' and they replied with one gutteral voice. He turned again to the missionary. 'You can stay with us if you like our ways. You can worship your own god. It is good that a man should worship the gods and the spirits of his fathers. Go back to your house so that you may not be hurt. Our anger is great but we have held it down so that we can talk to you.'

Mr Smith said to his interpreter: 'Tell them to go away from here. This is the house of God and I will not live to see it desecrated.'

Okeke interpreted wisely to the spirits and leaders of Umuofia: 'The white man says he is happy you have come to him with your grievances, like friends. He will be happy if you leave the matter in his hands.'

'We cannot leave the matter in his hands because he does not understand our customs, just as we do not understand his. We say he is foolish because he does not know our ways, and perhaps he says we are foolish because we do not know his. Let him go away.'

Mr Smith stood his ground. But he could not save his church. When the *egwugwu* went away the red-earth church which Mr Brown had built was a pile of earth and ashes. And for the moment the spirit of the clan was pacified.

Chapter Twenty-Three

For the first time in many years Okonkwo had a feeling that was akin to happiness. The times which had altered so unaccountably during his exile seemed to be coming round again. The clan which had turned false on him appeared to be making amends.

He had spoken violently to his clansmen when they had met in the market-place to decide on their action. And they had listened to him with respect. It was like the good old days again, when a warrior was a warrior. Although they had not agreed to kill the missionary or drive away the Christians, they had agreed to do something substantial. And they had done it. Okonkwo was almost happy again.

◆

For two days after the destruction of the church, nothing happened. Every man in Umuofia went about armed with a gun or a matchet. They would not be caught unawares, like the men of Abame.

Then the District Commissioner returned from his tour. Mr Smith went immediately to him and they had a long discussion. The men of Umuofia did not take any notice of this, and if they did, they thought it was not important. The missionary often went to see his brother white man. There was nothing strange in that.

Three days later the District Commissioner sent his sweet-tongued messenger to the leaders of Umuofia asking them to meet him in his headquarters. That also was not strange. He often asked them to hold such palavers, as he called them. Okonkwo was among the six leaders he invited.

Okonkwo warned the others to be fully armed. 'An Umuofia man does not refuse a call,' he said. 'He may refuse to do what he is asked;

he does not refuse to be asked. But the times have changed, and we must be fully prepared.'

And so the six men went to see the District Commissioner, armed with their matchets. They did not carry guns, for that would be unseemly. They were led into the court-house where the District Commissioner sat. He received them politely. They unslung their goatskin bags and their sheathed matchets, put them on the floor, and sat down.

'I have asked you to come,' began the Commissioner, 'because of what happened during my absence. I have been told a few things but I cannot believe them until I have heard your own side. Let us talk about it like friends and find a way of ensuring that it does not happen again.'

Ogbuefi Ekwueme rose to his feet and began to tell the story.

'Wait a minute,' said the Commissioner. 'I want to bring in my men so that they too can hear your grievances and take warning. Many of them come from distant places and although they speak your tongue they are ignorant of your customs. James! Go and bring in the men.' His interpreter left the court-room and soon returned with twelve men. They sat together with the men of Umuofia, and Ogbuefi Ekwueme began again to tell the story of how Enoch murdered an *egwugwu*.

It happened so quickly that the six men did not see it coming. There was only a brief scuffle, too brief even to allow the drawing of a sheathed matchet. The six men were handcuffed and led into the guardroom.

'We shall not do you any harm,' said the District Commissioner to them later, 'if only you agree to co-operate with us. We have brought a peaceful administration to you and your people so that you may be happy. If any man ill-treats you we shall come to your rescue. But we will not allow you to ill-treat others. We have a court of law where we judge cases and administer justice just as it is done in my own country under a great queen. I have brought you here because you joined together to molest others, to burn people's houses and their place of worship. That must not happen in the dominion of our queen, the most powerful ruler in the world. I have decided that you will pay a fine of two hundred bags of cowries. You will be released as soon as you agree to this and undertake to collect that fine from your people. What do you say to that?'

The six men remained sullen and silent and the Commissioner left them for a while. He told the court messengers, when he left the guardroom, to treat the men with respect because they were the leaders of Umuofia. They said, 'Yes, sir,' and saluted.

As soon as the District Commissioner left, the head messenger, who was also the prisoners' barber, took down his razor and shaved off all the hair on the men's heads. They were still handcuffed, and they just sat and moped.

'Who is the chief among you?' the court messenger asked in jest. 'We see that every pauper wears the anklet of title in Umuofia. Does it cost as much as ten cowries?'

The six men ate nothing throughout that day and the next. They were not even given any water to drink, and they could not go out to urinate or go into the bush when they were pressed. At night the messengers came in to taunt them and to knock their shaven heads together.

Even when the men were left alone they found no words to speak to one another. It was only on the third day, when they could no longer bear the hunger and the insults, that they began to talk about giving in.

'We should have killed the white man if you had listened to me,' Okonkwo snarled.

'We could have been in Umuru now waiting to be hanged,' someone said to him.

'Who wants to kill the white man?' asked a messenger who had just rushed in. Nobody spoke.

'You are not satisfied with your crime, but you must kill the white man on top of it.' He carried a strong stick, and he hit each man a few blows on the head and back. Okonkwo was choked with hate.

◆

As soon as the six men were locked up, court messengers went into Umuofia to tell the people that their leaders would not be released unless they paid a fine of two hundred and fifty bags of cowries.

'Unless you pay the fine immediately,' said their headman, 'we will take your leaders to Umuru before the big white man, and hang them.'

This story spread quickly through the villages, and was added to as it went. Some said that the men had already been taken to Umuru and would be hanged on the following day. Some said that their families would also be hanged. Others said that soldiers were already on their way to shoot the people of Umuofia as they had done in Abame.

It was the time of the full moon. But that night the voice of children was not heard. The village *ilo* where they always gathered for a moon-play was empty. The women of Iguedo did not meet in their secret enclosure to learn a new dance to be displayed later to the village. Young men who were always abroad in the moonlight kept their huts that night. Their manly voices were not heard on the village paths as they went to visit their friends and lovers. Umuofia was like a startled animal with ears erect, sniffing the silent, ominous air and not knowing which way to run.

The silence was broken by the village crier beating his sonorous *ogene*. He called every man in Umuofia, from the Akakanma age-group upwards, to a meeting in the market-place after the morning meal. He went from one end of the village to the other and walked all its breadth. He did not leave out any of the main footpaths.

Okonkwo's compound was like a deserted homestead. It was as if cold water had been poured on it. His family was all there, but everyone spoke in whispers. His daughter Ezinma had broken her twenty-eight day visit to the family of her future husband, and returned home when she heard that her father had been imprisoned, and was going to be hanged. As soon as she got home she went to Obierika to ask what the men of Umuofia were going to do about it. But Obierika had not been home since morning. His wives thought he had gone to a secret meeting. Ezinma was satisfied that something was being done.

On the morning after the village crier's appeal the men of Umuofia met in the market-place and decided to collect without delay two hundred and fifty bags of cowries to appease the white man. They did not know that fifty bags would go to the court messengers, who had increased the fine for that purpose.

139

Chapter Twenty-Four

Okonkwo and his fellow prisoners were set free as soon as the fine was paid. The District Commissioner spoke to them again about the great queen, and about peace and good government. But the men did not listen. They just sat and looked at him and at his interpreter. In the end they were given back their bags and sheathed matchets and told to go home. They rose and left the court-house. They neither spoke to anyone nor among themselves.

The court-house, like the church, was built a little way outside the village. The footpath that linked them was a very busy one because it also led to the stream, beyond the court. It was open and sandy. Footpaths were open and sandy in the dry season. But when the rains came the bush grew thick on either side and closed in on the path. It was now dry season.

As they made their way to the village the six men met women and children going to the stream with their waterpots. But the men wore such heavy and fearsome looks that the women and children did not say '*nno*' or 'welcome' to them, but edged out of the way to let them pass. In the village little groups of men joined them until they became a sizeable company. They walked silently. As each of the six men got to his compound, he turned in, taking some of the crowd with him. The village was astir in a silent, suppressed way.

Ezinma had prepared some food for her father as soon as news spread that the six men would be released. She took it to him in his *obi*. He ate absent-mindedly. He had no appetite; he only ate to please her. His male relations and friends had gathered in his *obi*, and Obierika was urging him to eat. Nobody else spoke, but they noticed the long stripes on Okonkwo's back where the warder's whip had cut into his flesh.

◆

The village crier was abroad again in the night. He beat his iron gong and announced that another meeting would be held in the morning. Everyone knew that Umuofia was at last going to speak its mind about the things that were happening.

Okonkwo slept very little that night. The bitterness in his heart was now mixed with a kind of child-like excitment. Before he had gone to bed he had brought down his war dress, which he had not touched since his return from exile. He had shaken out his smoked raffia skirt and examined his tall feather head-gear and his shield. They were all satisfactory, he had thought.

As he lay on his bamboo bed he thought about the treatment he had received in the white man's court, and he swore vengeance. If Umuofia decided on war, all would be well. But if they chose to be cowards he would go out and avenge himself. He thought about wars in the past. The noblest, he thought, was the war against Isike. In those days Okudo was still alive. Okudo sang a war song in a way that no other man could. He was not a fighter, but his voice turned every man into a lion.

'Worthy men are no more,' Okonkwo sighed as he remembered those days. 'Isike will never forget how we slaughtered them in that war. We killed twelve of their men and they killed only two of ours. Before the end of the fourth market week they were suing for peace. Those were days when men were men.'

As he thought of these things he heard the sound of the iron gong in the distance. He listened carefully, and could just hear the crier's voice. But it was very faint. He turned on his bed and his back hurt him. He ground his teeth. The crier was drawing nearer and nearer until he passed by Okonkwo's compound.

'The greatest obstacle in Umuofia,' Okonkwo thought bitterly, 'is that coward, Egonwanne. His sweet tongue can change fire into cold ash. When he speaks he moves our men to impotence. If they had ignored his womanish wisdom five years ago, we would not have come to this.' He ground his teeth. 'Tomorrow he will tell them that our fathers never fought a "war of blame". If they listen to him I shall leave them and plan my own revenge.'

The crier's voice had once more become faint, and the distance had taken the harsh edge off his iron gong. Okonkwo turned from one side to the other and derived a kind of pleasure from the pain his back gave him. 'Let Egonwanne talk about a "war of blame" tomorrow and I shall show him my back and head.' He ground his teeth.

◆

The market-place began to fill as soon as the sun rose. Obierika was waiting in his *obi* when Okonkwo came along and called him. He hung his goatskin bag and his sheathed matchet on his shoulder and went out to join him. Obierika's hut was close to the road and he saw every man who passed to the market-place. He had exchanged greetings with many who had already passed that morning.

When Okonkwo and Obierika got to the meeting-place there were already so many people that if one threw up a grain of sand it would not find its way to the earth again. And many more people were coming from every quarter of the nine villages. It warmed Okonkwo's heart to see such strength of numbers. But he was looking for one man in particular, the man whose tongue he dreaded and despised so much.

'Can you see him?' he asked Obierika.

'Who?'

'Egonwanne,' he said, his eyes roving from one corner of the huge market-place to the other. Most of the men were seated on goatskins on the ground. A few of them sat on wooden stools they had brought with them.

'No,' said Obierika, casting his eyes over the crowd. 'Yes, there he is, under the silk-cotton tree. Are you afraid he would convince us not to fight?'

'Afraid? I do not care what he does to *you*. I despise him and those who listen to him. I shall fight alone if I choose.'

They spoke at the top of their voices because everybody was talking, and it was like the sound of a great market.

'I shall wait till he has spoken,' Okonkwo thought. 'Then I shall speak.'

'But how do you know he will speak against war?' Obierika asked after a while.

'Because I know he is a coward,' said Okonkwo. Obierika did not hear the rest of what he said because at that moment somebody touched his shoulder from behind and he turned round to shake hands and exchange greetings with five or six friends. Okonkwo did not turn around even though he knew the voices. He was in no mood to exchange greetings. But one of the men touched him and asked about the people of his compound.

'They are well,' he replied without interest.

The first man to speak to Umuofia that morning was Okika, one of the six who had been imprisoned. Okika was a great man and an orator. But he did not have the booming voice which a first speaker must use to establish silence in the assembly of the clan. Onyeka had such a voice; and so he was asked to salute Umuofia before Okika began to speak.

'*Umuofia kwenu!*' he bellowed, raising his left arm and pushing the air with his open hand.

'*Yaa!*' roared Umuofia.

'*Umuofia kwenu!*' he bellowed again, and again and again, facing a new direction each time. And the crowd answered, '*Yaa!*'

There was immediate silence as though cold water had been poured on a roaring flame.

Okika sprang to his feet and also saluted his clansmen four times. Then he began to speak:

'You all know why we are here, when we ought to be building our barns or mending our huts, when we should be putting our compounds in order. My father used to say to me: "Whenever you see a toad jumping in broad daylight, then know that something is after its life." When I saw you all pouring into this meeting from all the quarters of our clan so early in the morning, I knew that something was after our life.' He paused for a brief moment and then began again:

'All our gods are weeping. Idemili is weeping. Ogwugwu is weeping. Agbala is weeping, and all the others. Our dead fathers are weeping because of the shameful sacrilege they are suffering and the abomination we have all seen with our eyes.' He stopped again to steady his trembling voice.

'This is a great gathering. No clan can boast of greater numbers or greater valour. But are we all here? I ask you: Are all the sons of Umuofia with us here?' A deep murmur swept through the crowd.

143

'They are not,' he said. 'They have broken the clan and gone their several ways. We who are here this morning have remained true to our fathers, but our brothers have deserted us and joined a stranger to soil their fatherland. If we fight the stranger we shall hit our brothers and perhaps shed the blood of a clansman. But we must do it. Our fathers never dreamt of such a thing, they never killed their brothers. But a white man never came to them. So we must do what our fathers would never have done. Eneke the bird was asked why he was always on the wing and he replied: "Men have learnt to shoot without missing their mark and I have learnt to fly without perching on a twig." We must root out this evil. And if our brothers take the side of evil we must root them out too. And we must do it *now*. We must bale this water now that it is only ankle-deep . . .'

At this point here was a sudden stir in the crowd and every eye was turned in one direction. There was a sharp bend in the road that led from the market-place to the white man's court, and to the stream beyond it. And so no one had seen the approach of the five court messengers until they had come round the bend, a few paces from the edge of the crowd. Okonkwo was sitting at the edge.

He sprang to his feet as soon as he saw who it was. He confronted the head messenger, trembling with hate, unable to utter a word. The man was fearless and stood his ground, his four men lined up behind him.

In that brief moment the world seemed to stand still, waiting. There was utter silence. The men of Umuofia were merged into the mute backcloth of trees and giant creepers, waiting.

The spell was broken by the head messenger. 'Let me pass!' he ordered.

'What do you want here?'

'The white man whose power you know too well has ordered this meeting to stop.'

In a flash Okonkwo drew his matchet. The messenger crouched to avoid the blow. It was useless. Okonkwo's matchet decended twice and the man's head lay beside his uniformed body.

The waiting backcloth jumped into tumultuous life and the meeting was stopped. Okonkwo stood looking at the dead man. He knew that Umuofia would not go to war. He knew because they had let the other messengers escape. They had broken into tumult instead of action. He discerned fright in that tumult. He heard voices asking: 'Why did he do it?'

He wiped his matchet on the sand and went away.

Chapter Twenty-Five

When the District Commissioner arrived at Okonkwo's compound at the head of an armed band of soldiers and court messengers he found a small crowd of men sitting wearily in the *obi*. He commanded them to come outside, and they obeyed without a murmur.

'Which among you is called Okonkwo?' he asked through his interpreter.

'He is not here,' replied Obierika.

'Where is he?'

'He is not here!'

The Commissioner became angry and red in the face. He warned the men that unless they produced Okonkwo forthwith he would lock them all up. The men murmured among themselves, and Obierika spoke again.

'We can take you where he is, and perhaps your men will help us.'

The Commissioner did not understand what Obierika meant when he said, 'Perhaps your men will help us.' One of the most infuriating habits of these people was their love of superfluous words, he thought.

Obierika with five or six others led the way. The Commissioner and his men followed, their firearms held at the ready. He had warned Obierika that if he and his men played any monkey tricks they would be shot. And so they went.

There was a small bush behind Okonkwo's compound. The only opening into this bush from the compound was a little round hole in the red-earth wall through which fowls went in and out in their endless search for food. The hole would not let a man through. It was to this bush that Obierika led the Commissioner and his men. They skirted round the compound, keeping close to the wall. The only sound they made was with their feet as they crushed dry leaves.

Then they came to the tree from which Okonkwo's body was dangling, and they stopped dead.

'Perhaps your men can help us bring him down and bury him,' said Obierika. 'We have sent for strangers from another village to do it for us, but they may be a long time coming.'

The District Commissioner changed instantaneously. The resolute administrator in him gave way to the student of primitive customs.

'Why can't you take him down yourselves?' he asked.

'It is against our custom,' said one of the men. 'It is an abomination for a man to take his own life. It is an offence against the Earth, and a man who commits it will not be buried by his clansmen. His body is evil, and only strangers may touch it. That is why we ask your people to bring him down, because you are strangers.'

'Will you bury him like any other man?' asked the Commissioner.

'We cannot bury him. Only strangers can. We shall pay your men to do it. When he has been buried we will then do our duty by him. We shall make sacrifices to cleanse the desecrated land.'

Obierika, who had been gazing steadily at his friend's dangling body, turned suddenly to the District Commissioner and said ferociously: 'That man was one of the greatest men in Umuofia. You drove him to kill himself; and now he will be buried like a dog . . .'

He could not say any more. His voice trembled and choked his words.

'Shut up!' shouted one of the messengers, quite unnecessarily.

'Take down the body,' the Commissioner ordered his chief messenger, 'and bring it and all these people to court.'

'Yes, sah,' the messenger said, saluting.

The Commissioner went away, taking three or four of the soldiers with him. In the many years in which he had toiled to bring civilization to different parts of Africa he had learnt a number of things. One of them was that a District Commissioner must never attend to such undignified details as cutting down a dead man from the tree. Such attention would give the natives a poor opinion of him. In the book which he planned to write he would stress that point. As he walked back to the court he thought about that book. Every day brought him some new material. The story of this man who had killed a messenger and hanged himself would make interesting reading. One could almost write a whole chapter on him. Perhaps not a whole chapter but a

147

reasonable paragraph, at any rate. There was so much else to include, and one must be firm in cutting out details. He had already chosen the title of the book, after much thought: *The Pacification of the Primitive Tribes of the Lower Niger.*